"What are you

"That's my line," Sean replied. "And at the risk of sounding like one of the three bears, I'll point out that someone has been sleeping in my bed, and she's still here."

"Your bed?" Erica said. "This is my compartment. If you don't get out this minute, I'm going to buzz for the car attendant."

"Be my guest," Sean dared her, fishing a ticket out of his pocket. "You're going to feel awfully silly when I show him this and he bounces you out on that cute little behind of yours."

Erica looked at the ticket. "Eric S. O'Leary," she read aloud. "That's your name?" It was also her name—almost. Suddenly she realized that the computer must have spit out his reservation when she told the ticket agent her name. There hadn't been a cancellation, only a crazy mix-up. Now what was she going to do?

"Everybody calls me Sean," he said. "That's what the *S* stands for. I don't suppose you'd want to show me your ticket."

"Not particularly," she said, settling back on the pillow. "I'm comfortable and it would be extremely inconvenient." *And it would take him about five seconds to figure out what had happened.*

He shrugged. "Suit yourself." Then he reached for the waistband of his slacks.

Glenda Sanders fell in love while doing research for *Midnight Train from Georgia*—with train travel, that is. "I was in a tiny room, all alone, serenaded by the click of the wheels and rocked by the motion of the train," she says. "There was no phone, no one expecting me to cook dinner, no basset hound howling to be taken for a walk. Unfortunately, I didn't come across a gorgeous man claiming we shared the same sleeper, either. I guess you can't get all the breaks!"

Books by Glenda Sanders

Glenda Sanders
MIDNIGHT TRAIN FROM GEORGIA

Harlequin Books

TORONTO • NEW YORK • LONDON
AMSTERDAM • PARIS • SYDNEY • HAMBURG
STOCKHOLM • ATHENS • TOKYO • MILAN
MADRID • WARSAW • BUDAPEST • AUCKLAND

The author acknowledges with gratitude the patient guidance of Baltimore resident and fellow author Binnie Braunstein, who played hostess, chauffeur, tour guide and fabric consultant during my visit to Baltimore. I hope your life is filled with furry beasts and happy endings.

And to Officer H. at the Baltimore County Police Department: Thank you for answering questions from a frantic writer who hopes never to experience an arrest firsthand. You and your fellow officers have my respect and admiration for taking on a tough job.

ISBN 0-373-25703-1

MIDNIGHT TRAIN FROM GEORGIA

1

"CHECK OUT the strawberry blonde at the deli counter."

"I have been," Sean O'Leary told the man seated next to him. He'd been hoping no one else would notice her. "I don't think she's with our group." He would have remembered if he'd seen her before.

"If I weren't in a monogamous relationship," Michael mused aloud.

"But you are," Sean reminded him.

"You're not," Michael said. "Why not try to strike up a conversation? She's not wearing a ring. I can live vicariously."

"What's the use?" Sean said. "It's after midnight." The train had been almost an hour late pulling out of Savannah.

"So? You turn into a pumpkin at midnight, or something?"

"It's just a little late to be striking up a conversation." *Too bad he hadn't seen her earlier.*

"Hell, Sean, with that attitude, you might as well not have booked a sleeper."

"I booked a sleeper because I have to be in Judge Finkbein's courtroom tomorrow afternoon," Sean said.

"Finkbein?" Mike said. "Jeez, if you're squaring off against Finkbein tomorrow, you owe it to yourself to give the blonde a try."

Sean was listening to Mike, but his attention was focused on two men in their group who were eyeing the woman with drunken intensity. Two *married* men who'd both had too much to drink and were on the verge of making total asses of themselves if someone didn't beat them to it.

"You have a point," Sean said, rising. "Even a condemned man gets a final meal." It was only a matter of time before someone gave the strawberry blonde the rush. Better one sober single man over two married, obnoxious drunks.

Of course, the magnanimity of his rescue would probably totally escape the attention of the lady.

Up close, she was shorter than he'd have estimated from across the car. The top of her head was an inch or two below his shoulder, which would put her on the short side of five-four or so. She'd pulled a caffeine-free diet cola from the cooler case, and was deliberating over the rack of candy bars near the cashier's stand.

"Caffeine free, huh?" Sean asked.

"Caffeine makes me hyper and I need—" she turned and looked at him before adding "—to get some sleep tonight." Her soft features blended into an interesting face—until she smiled. The smile, and a small dimple that appeared just to the right of her mouth, transformed "interesting" into "fascinating."

Sean swallowed as his heart skipped a beat. She hadn't meant for the comment to be suggestive, he was sure, any more than he'd expected to respond to her like a testosterone-charged teenager. He drew in a breath and released it slowly, a calming device he frequently used in the courtroom, then returned her smile. "A glass of wine would relax you."

"Wine? I don't think—"

"The bar's still open," he said. "Just one?"

She considered the invitation before replying haltingly, "Thanks, but . . . no, thank you."

Sean frowned charmingly and bent to speak confidentially, "I didn't want to have to tell you this, but you see those two shady-looking characters over there?"

She followed his gaze. "The ones in the Kiss Me. I'm An Irish Attorney sweatshirts?"

Sean nodded. "They're the real reason I came over here. You see, they've had a lot to drink and they've been staring at you ever since you came in. I thought if you went to the bar with me, they wouldn't come over and bother you."

Her lips compressed in irritation.

"They're pretty lecherous types," Sean pressed.

"They're attorneys," she said, as though that explained everything.

Sean grimaced. "You aren't with the association, are you?"

"Association?" It was obvious she had no idea what he was talking about.

"The Association of Irish-American Attorneys," he said. "We just took in the St. Patrick's Day parade in Savannah."

"I'm half-Irish, but I'd rather be a carnival barker than an attorney," she said sharply. "So, while I appreciate your concern, I'm really not interested in a drink. It's late and . . . I'm not in a drinking mood. If you'll excuse me—"

She turned away from him abruptly to pay the cashier for her soda and hastily exited the lounge car. Just when she'd thought the longest, worst day of her life couldn't possibly get any more frustrating, a gorgeous man tries to pick her up when she's too exhausted and distracted to think about getting acquainted. And to make matters worse, he's a lawyer.

A lawyer! Wasn't having to rush to her grandmother's deathbed bad enough—did she have to get there on a train filled with lawyers?

Thank goodness she'd been able to get a sleeper. With what she was facing when she reached Baltimore, she desperately needed privacy on this trip. And comfort.

Her compartment was three cars back. Once inside, Erica kicked off her shoes, wiggled her toes, leaned back in the seat and sighed, offering silent thanks to whoever had canceled their reservation at the last moment. Pressing her forehead against the window, she peered at the stars dotting the blue-blackness of the midnight sky. How many times had she and her grandmother looked up at the stars, her grandmother pointing to constellations, calling them by their mysterious Latin names and telling about the ancient gods for whom they'd been named?

She blinked back a tear, afraid that if she let even one escape, the dam inside her would burst. Her grandmother was dying. The message to call her grandmother's doctor had been on her answering machine when she'd gotten home from work. Her grandmother had no more than a few days, a week at most.

Erica had immediately launched into action, reserving a seat on the train, packing, doing laundry, arranging for her neighbor to bring in the mail and watch her cat while she was away. Now, after all the rushing around and the frantic race to catch the evening train, she was finally on her way. There was nothing more she could do about her grandmother until she reached Baltimore. Nothing—except think and pray. Think of all the things she should have said through the years, all the thank-yous and apologies that had gone unspoken. Pray that by the time she arrived, her grandmother would be alert enough to hear and understand her.

She opened the packaged "lunch" Gary had given her and the canned soft drink she'd just bought. Good ole Gary. How like him to be both thoughtful and pragmatic. Food had been the last thing on her mind as she rushed around trying to make the train. But now that she'd slowed down, the crackers, cold cuts and cheese were a godsend.

And how like Gary to call and offer to drive her anywhere she needed to go. He would have probably driven her all the way to Baltimore but she'd asked merely that he drive her the fifty miles into Savannah to catch the train, since she had been unable to book a flight. She'd fidgeted all the way, worrying that she'd forgotten something essential even as she anxiously scribbled out lesson plans for Gary, the vice principal at the school where she taught third grade, to give to the substitute teacher who'd take over her classes.

Spooning the chocolate pudding dessert into her mouth, Erica reflected that she had gotten the better end of the bargain when she and Gary, after dating briefly, had chosen friendship over romance. Gary always came through when she needed a friend, sometimes even before she realized she needed one.

After finishing her meal, Erica pulled her bed down from the wall and bolted it into place, pleasantly surprised at how much wider it was than the sleepers in coach class, which she normally traveled. The mattress was thicker, too. Good. She could use every shred of comfort she could get tonight.

With the bed down, the compartment was narrow, restricting her movement as she changed into her flannel nightgown. Once she was covered by enough flannel to keep a nun chaste, she slid the metal door halfway open so she wouldn't feel so confined. The dark, Velcro-closed draperies beyond provided more than ample privacy while she ran a steaming washcloth over her face and brushed her teeth at the small sink.

Wearily, she climbed into the bed, and shoved the rigid plastic window cover up. For several minutes she stared into the velvet night while memories of past trips played through her mind—all the trips from Georgia, where she'd lived with her father, to Baltimore, where she'd gone for her court-enforced visits with her grandmother. Usually, her grandmother had come for her, and they'd made the trip back to Baltimore together on the train. Her grandmother had called their travels "grand adventures."

"We'll have another grand adventure as soon as school's out for the summer," she'd whisper in Erica's ear before grudgingly turning her over to her father.

Erica closed the window and rolled onto her side, turning her head away from the night-light next to the window and pulling the covers up over her shoulders. Spring break, seven weeks of her summer vacation, the week between Christmas and New Year's Day and no less than five weekends a year by arrangement with the custodial parent—it had taken a cadre of lawyers and judges over the years to come up with justice for a grandmother who disliked and mistrusted the man her only child had married.

Although everyone tried to shield Erica from their legal feuding, the enmity between the two people she loved had seeped into her life. Her father had prepared her for the court-directed visits with ill-concealed resentment, and her grandmother's reluctance to return Erica to her father had been hidden beneath a thin veneer of civility. Through the years, Erica's attitude toward being fought over had run the gamut from bewilderment to bitterness, particularly when her "grand adventures" with her grandmother had widened the gap between her and the step-siblings from her father's second and third marriages. It wasn't until she approached adulthood and her father's messy divorce from his third wife had turned her life upside down that she had come to appreciate the stability her grandmother represented in her life.

Erica choked back a sob. *So many years! Oh, Gram, I didn't understand that it was because you loved me. That you felt you had to do what you did in order to protect me. Why couldn't I have seen it sooner?*

She could almost feel her grandmother's gentle fingers brushing her forehead, almost hear her grandmother's sweet voice answering, "Because you were a child, of course. You couldn't be expected to understand then. The important thing is that you understand now."

Erica closed her eyes, hoping that she would have time to stroke her grandmother's forehead soothingly and tell her that, finally, she understood. To thank her for being there to watch out for her, for not giving up, for filling her life with grand adventures. To thank her... for everything.

The motion of the train was like a rocking cradle, the *cla-click, cla-click* of the wheels a lullaby. Erica snuggled into the warm bedding and slept.

STIFLING A YAWN with a soft groan, Sean laced his fingers together, extended his arms above his head and stretched. "I'm beat. I'm going to call it a night."

"Party pooper!" Michael teased. "It's only—"

"Two o'clock in the morning," Sean said, rising to leave. "I'm not used to these wild weekends anymore."

"Whatever you paid for that sleeper, I'll double it." Michael shielded a yawn with his hand.

"Not a chance," Sean said. "The last time I slept in a coach seat, I had kinks in inconvenient places." The drop-down sleeper was small compared to his king-size bed at home, but at least it was flat and soft.

"As if anyone could get any sleep in the car we're in, anyway," Michael grumbled. "They're still partying heartily."

"See you at breakfast," Sean said without a lot of sympathy. Fatigue rode on his shoulders as he moved from car to car, each quieter than the last. *Thank goodness!* Four days of noise, silliness and chicanery had left him craving peace and quiet.

He found his compartment easily enough. Evidently the car attendant had gone in to make the bed, because the outside curtains were pulled and the metal door was halfway closed. He waited for his eyes to adjust to the frail glow cast by the night-light before attempting to locate the switch for the overhead light. When he finally made the move, his foot collided with something in the center of the floor, and as he regained his balance, he caught sight of the bed in his peripheral vision. His mind identified the form of a human being resting there.

A woman, he discovered after taking a closer look. Blond hair splayed across the small pillow, and the blanket molded around a distinctively female hip.

His guts constricted as he stared at the sleeping figure. He must have entered the wrong sleeper—how could he have made such a mistake? If this woman woke up and found a strange man in her room—

He shook his head as if to clear it. He hadn't made a mistake. He'd checked the number on both the car and the room. This was his compartment, and the sleeping woman was in *his* bed.

So what was a woman doing there?

With the softest of sighs, the woman in question shifted in her sleep, settling with her face toward him. Sean swallowed a gasp when he recognized the blonde from the lounge car.

Realization dawned with lightning-strike intensity. *The privacy door hadn't been latched.* He'd been set up—big time. What woman would go to sleep without locking every door within reach?

Only a woman who wanted to make it easy for him to find her. Sean looked at that pretty face, angelic in repose, and fumed.

"Check out the strawberry blonde at the deli counter." Indeed! Michael and this little strawberry shortcake must have

cooked up this whole scenario. Who else could have given her the number of his compartment? Michael must have been close to convulsions holding back laughter, knowing Sean would find her in his bed after she brushed him off in the deli.

Sean set his jaw. He was going to inflict bodily harm on Michael the next time he saw him. But first, he had to deal with this unlikely interloper.

He scowled at her, wondering who she was. He was fairly certain she wasn't with the association. So who was she? A hooker? He discounted that possibility immediately. Not unless she was damned good at appearing unhookerish. No, she was just some woman Michael had run into. She'd probably given him a sob story about wishing she had a sleeper. She might even be a stowaway, hiding in his room without a ticket.

The situation was not without possibilities. If he hadn't been partying for four days and didn't have to face Finkbein tomorrow, he might have seen the humor in it. He might even have been tempted to play along. But he needed a good night's sleep. In private.

With a moment's regret for what might have been, he raised his hand and gave her shapely rump a whap. "Okay, Shortcakes! Game's over. It would have been fun, but—"

She awoke with a dazed groan that turned into a gasp of alarm. If he hadn't been so certain he'd been set up, he would have believed her incredulity; instead, he attributed her stellar performance to the natural reaction of a person rudely awakened from a deep sleep.

"What are you doing here?" she asked, instinctively clutching the bedding to her chest.

"That's my line," he replied. "At the risk of sounding like Baby Bear, I'll point out that someone has been sleeping in my bed, and she's still there."

"*Your* bed?" she said. "This is my compartment. And if you don't get out right this minute, I'm going to buzz for the car attendant."

"Be my guest," Sean dared, gesturing toward the call button. Spying the overhead light switch, he flicked it on, and light flooded the small enclosure. He fished his ticket from his pocket. "You're going to feel awfully silly when I show him this and he bounces you out on that cute little behind of yours."

"Is that a ticket?"

"Thought that might wake you up," he said.

"For this room?" She sounded dismayed.

"I wouldn't be here if it wasn't. So why don't you just climb out of my bed and—"

"Let me see it."

Sean held up the ticket, but when she reached to take it, he snatched it away. "Look, but don't touch."

Her features tightened with irritation. "I wasn't going to *steal* it."

"Technically, by occupying that sleeper, to which I hold a ticket granting me exclusive right of occupation between Savannah and Baltimore, you are already stealing it—or at least, usurping the exclusive privilege it grants me."

"Attorneys!" she grumbled. Then, as he held up the ticket again, she read aloud, "Eric S. O'Leary." Her eyes fixed on his face in surprise. "That's your name?"

It was also her name—almost.

"Same as me dear old dad's," he said, adopting an exaggerated Irish accent.

"Oh," she said, unable to keep her disappointment out of the word. Eric S. O'Leary. Erica S. O'Leary. The computer must have spit out *his* reservation when she told the ticket agent *her* name. There hadn't been a cancellation at all, only a crazy mix-up based on an uncanny coincidence.

"Everyone calls me Sean," he said. "That's what the S is for."

"Well, *Sean*, obviously there's been some mistake, because I also have a ticket for this sleeper."

"I don't suppose you'd want to show it to me."

"Not particularly," she said, settling back on the pillow. "I'm comfortable, and getting it would be extremely inconvenient." And it would take him about five seconds to figure out what had happened and deduce that he was the rightful occupant of the compartment, since he'd bought his ticket first. For all she knew, in the state she was in when she'd given the ticket agent her name, her ticket could have Eric instead of Erica on it and she wouldn't have noticed.

For a moment, he looked as though he might argue, but finally he shrugged. "Suit yourself."

Erica felt some of the tension ease from her shoulders and neck. He was going to leave without an argument.

Or so she thought. Instead, he opened his briefcase and took out a toothbrush and travel-size tube of toothpaste. Then he turned the knob that freed the sink from the upright position and turned on the water. He squeezed a strip of toothpaste onto the bristles of the brush.

Erica watched him run the brush under the tap to wet it before poking it into his mouth. "What do you think you're doing?" she asked in the tone of voice she saved for unruly students.

"Brussing muh eeth," he said, his mouth full of lather. He plucked a paper cup from the dispenser above the sink, filled it and rinsed.

"Do you always carry a toothbrush in your briefcase?"

Sean spat out the rinse water. "Only when I travel."

"*Now* what are you doing?" Erica asked, although it was perfectly obvious that he was taking off his shirt.

"Undressing," he said, folding his shirt with meticulous care.

"Well, stop it this instant!"

He cocked his head. "You sound like a schoolteacher."

Erica's lips compressed briefly in irritation before she replied tautly, "That's totally irrelevant."

His chuckle grated over her nerves. "You *are* a schoolteacher! I love it! Where did Michael link up with you?"

"Who's Michael?"

He grinned. "Nice touch, Shortcakes, but you don't have to pretend. I know the two of you cooked this up."

"You're delusional," she said. "I don't know who you're talking about, and I haven't cooked anything up with anyone."

"He's the only one who could have given you the number of my sleeper."

"The ticket agent gave me the number of *my* sleeper," she said. "And I didn't cook anything up with him. I just bought a ticket." It wasn't the whole truth, as she knew it now, but it was the truth.

He balanced on one leg, folding the other across his knee, and removed his right loafer, then reversed the process. A moment later, he reached for the waistband of his slacks.

"What are you doing now?" Erica screeched as the grate of the fly zipper reverberated through the compartment.

"Taking off my pants."

"Don't you dare!"

He pushed down his pants, pausing as he stepped out of them to say, "I always take off my pants before I get into bed."

Erica's jaw dropped when she saw the boxer shorts he had on. "Do you always wear underwear with shamrocks and leprechauns on it?"

Sean looked down at the boxers and frowned. "Only when my housekeeper forgets to do my laundry before I take a trip.

I was going to duck into a department store to buy some briefs, but I saw these on a street vendor's cart and couldn't resist."

"They're ridiculous," Erica said, noting that his body wasn't. His chest was broad and beautifully muscled and generously sprinkled with hair that tapered down a reasonably flat midriff before tucking into the elastic waist of the boxers.

"Probably," he agreed. "But I'm not sure I'd be too quick to point that out if I was wearing a nightie with fuzzy little sheep all over it."

Erica pulled the covers up to her chin again and snapped, "I wasn't dressing to impress anyone."

"Trust me, Shortcakes. I'm not impressed."

"Why don't you just leave," she groaned.

"Because I need a good night's sleep."

"Well, you're not going to get it in this sleeper."

"I don't know why not. I have a ticket that says I'm entitled to sleep in that bed."

"So do I," Erica said. "And I'm already in this bed." She wiggled under the covers and tried to sound confident. "You know what they say—possession is nine-tenths of the law."

"I'll bet your dear old granny taught you that."

The cavalier mention of her grandmother cut Erica to the quick. "Yes," she said. "She did."

"Well, granny and I don't practice the same law," he said. "My law is that I have a ticket. I also have a tough afternoon in court tomorrow. So I am getting in that bed."

For a man wearing nothing but a pair of leprechaun-and-shamrock boxer shorts, he spoke with an impressive amount of authority. "But—"

"You, on the other hand, may or may not have a ticket, which means that you may or may not have a right to be here. And in the immortal words of dear old Rhett, 'Frankly, my dear, I don't give a damn.' The bottom line is that I'm getting in that bed. Whether or not you wish to remain there is up to you."

"You *can't* be serious," she said.

He grinned. "Aisle or window, Shortcakes?"

2

ERICA DECIDED to try another tack. Sighing heavily, she said, "Look. There's been a mix-up, and I'm sorry, but you can't expect . . . I mean—" Holding the bedding against her chest, she sat up and dropped her legs off the edge of the bed. "You're insane!"

"Are you leaving, or just making it easy for me to get next to the window?"

"I don't even *know* you!" she said. "I'm not—"

"If you're worried about being molested, you're worrying unnecessarily. If that gown is as long as it is high, James Bond couldn't get inside it." *Although . . . given encouragement, he'd be willing to try.*

Erica had never been as tempted to strike a person in her life. "I don't need this!" she said, hopping out of the bed as he climbed in. "Not tonight, of all nights."

"I take it you're leaving?" he said, gloating.

She answered with a scowl. "I—" She stopped and swallowed. "The day I'm facing tomorrow isn't going to be easy for me, either. I could use the rest. Won't you—"

He was already stretching out and settling in. Rolling onto his side, he pushed up on one elbow and patted the bedding next to him. "We *could* share."

"You *could* be a compassionate human being and let me have the room," she countered.

"I'm compassionate," he said. "I offered to share."

Erica crossed her hands over her waist and frowned.

"There's plenty of room," he said. "If we scrunch."

"I never...*scrunch* with strangers," Erica said, opening the small closet and taking out her skirt and sweater. *Especially gorgeous Irish lawyers wearing leprechaun underwear.* She cast him a hostile look. "At least have the decency to turn your head so I can get dressed."

"You didn't turn your head when I got undressed."

And what a big mistake that had been! The shamrock skivvies weren't the only thing that had left a lasting impression in her mind. With a sniff of impatience, she turned her back to Sean. Using the long gown as a privacy shroud, she pulled on her clothes, aware of Sean O'Leary's eyes on her as she moved. At last, when she felt presentable enough to remove the gown so she could straighten her sweater properly, she rolled up the night wear and stuffed it into her carryall. She yanked the zipper closed, slung the strap over her shoulder and jammed her feet into her shoes.

"I wish I could say it'd been a pleasure meeting you," she said, "but my grandmother taught me it was wrong to lie."

"I'll leave the door ajar in case you change your mind," he said.

Change my mind! Erica fumed as she moved forward, car by car, imagining the people beyond the doors she passed, all of them sleeping comfortably, oblivious to all but the rocking of the train and the comfort of their beds. *They* hadn't been wrested from a sound sleep by a *lawyer* wearing leprechaun underwear. *They* hadn't been give a room in error. *They* weren't going to spend the night in a coach seat trying to sleep.

Their grandmothers weren't dying.

She grasped the handle of the door leading from the last sleeping car to the door of the lounge car, but instead of pulling the door open, she pressed her forehead against the cold metal and exhaled wearily. *It wasn't their fault her grandmother was dying. It was just . . . the way things were.*

Wearily, she entered the lounge car, involuntarily holding her breath against the miasmic cloud of smoke hovering over it. She walked up the narrow aisle in quick strides, avoiding eye contact with any of the men clustered in small groups nursing mixed drinks from the bar. One obnoxious lawyer was more than enough aggravation for any evening.

Having made it through the lounge car unmolested, she wasn't expecting to find mayhem in the coach car. She heard the commotion over the *clickety-clack* of the wheels even before the door was fully open. Inside, everyone seemed to be drinking beer from long-necked bottles, and a short, rotund man in a leprechaun costume was leading the group in a raucous Irish drinking ballad. Erica was just beginning to make sense of the bawdy lyrics, when she was approached by a man in one of the Kiss Me. I'm An Irish Attorney sweat-shirts she'd seen earlier.

"Ah, lass, come in, come in," he said, taking her elbow to escort her. "Don't be shy now. Join our celebration."

Nonplussed, Erica said, "I just . . ." *Wanted to find a seat where I could curl up and go to sleep,* she meant to say, but her voice trailed off as she realized the odds against that happening.

"Blarney stone! Blarney stone!" First one voice began the chant, and several others followed. "Blar-ney stone! Blar-ney stone!"

"Everyone who enters the car must kiss the Blarney stone," the man told her, leaning close to her ear to be heard over the chanting. "It's a tradition on this trip."

"But I'm not with your group," Erica said, wondering how soon she could get away from this mayhem.

"Doesn't matter," the man said. "Everyone's Irish for three days before and three days after St. Patrick's Day. Ah! Here's the Blarney stone now."

A jovial-looking man somewhere between fifty and sixty years old bowed from the waist in front of her and pointed to the top of his totally bald head. Blarney Stone had been written on his skin with a green marker. "Plant a big one right here, me *malvoureen*."

"Does your mother know you've been writing on your head?" she asked, provoking several ooo's from the people who'd turned to watch the spectacle.

"My mother doesn't even know I've *lost* my hair!" he said. "I usually wear a toupee."

"Come on and kiss the stone!" someone urged.

"You might as well just do it," said a female voice. The speaker was a tall, statuesque brunette wearing one of the Irish-attorney shirts. She smiled reassuringly. "This Blarney-stone business has been going on all weekend. It's harmless."

Deciding that being a good sport would be the shortest route to being left alone, Erica leaned over and kissed the man's head.

"What's your name, dearie?" asked the man dressed like a leprechaun.

"Erica," she replied.

"All right!" the leprechaun cried, raising his hands like a choirmaster. "Our newcomer's name is Erica, and she just kissed the Blarney stone."

Suddenly everyone was singing:

She kissed the Blarney stone!
She kissed the Blarney stone!
Now Erica is Irish, from her head down to her bone!

This ditty was followed by a round of applause.

"My head down to my bone?" Erica mused aloud.

The brunette gave a robust chuckle. "We're lawyers, not songwriters."

"Now that you're one of us, how about a green beer?" The offer came from her self-appointed escort.

"No," Erica said. "Thank you, but—"

"Just one?" the man cajoled.

"No. Really. I'm just passing through." Erica eased past him and left the car. She heaved a sigh of relief as she entered the next car and found it peacefully quiet and dark except for the pale security lights.

She was immediately approached by a car attendant who whispered, "Good evening, miss. May I ask where you're headed?"

"I'm trying to find an empty seat and get some sleep," Erica replied.

"I'll have to see your ticket."

With a sinking sensation, Erica took the ticket from the outside zipper pocket of her carryall and handed it to him. Holding it under a small flashlight, the attendant studied it a moment, then raised his gaze to Erica's face. "This ticket is for a sleeper."

"There was a mix-up," she said. "I was on the waiting list for a sleeper and when I bought my ticket, they called up someone else's reservation. His name is similar to mine, and—"

"You need to see the attendant in the sleeper car, then," he said.

"It's so late," Erica said. "Why can't I just find a seat and—"

"All our seats are assigned, and they're all occupied," he said.

"But there must be an empty seat somewhere," Erica said.

"Not between here and the front of the train," he said. "That's why I'm here—making sure no one comes forward and disturbs anybody."

"Then what—"

"You might find a place to sit in the car you just left," the attendant said. "The tour had the entire car, and some of them booked sleepers, as well, so there may be some empty seats. If they don't mind—"

"But they're partying."

He shook his head. "Yes, ma'am. They sure are. I've been working on trains for twenty-five years, and I don't recall many groups like that one. But if there's an empty seat on this train, it's in that car."

Erica's dismay must have shown on her face, because he said, sympathetically, "Sorry. That's the best advice I can give you. It's that, or go back to the sleeping-car attendant, but I don't know what he'd tell you that I haven't."

Erica thanked him and reluctantly returned to the car she'd just come from, hoping to slip in unnoticed. But the cry of "Blarney stone!" showed her the futility of that hope. The chant was quickly picked up by the crowd, and before she had a chance to react, the man with Blarney Stone written on his head was bowing in front of her.

"Again?" she asked.

"Every time someone comes into the car, he or she has to kiss the stone," came the reply.

Anxious to remove herself from the center of attention, she gave the slick pate a perfunctory kiss, and once more endured the inane ditty about kissing the stone.

"Change your mind about that beer?" It was the man who'd offered it to her earlier.

"No. Thank you. I—"

"Give it a break, Murphy," the tall brunette said. "She doesn't want a beer."

Erica cast her a grateful look. "I was hoping to find an empty seat somewhere."

"There's a seat by me," three men said simultaneously.

"Why sit when you can dance?" said a man who'd obviously had one too many green beers. He slung his arm across her shoulders clumsily.

"I never dance with men who have green tongues," Erica said, shrinking away from his advance.

"Oh, come on, honey. Haven't you heard about green tongues? They're the most talented kind." He closed his arms around her, trapping her.

Erica grabbed his arms and flung them away. "Don't 'honey' me, you drunken fool. I'm not your honey."

This scene provoked laughter from a couple of the men who'd been observing the drunken man's efforts. "Hey, Casey, give it up!" one of them said. "The lady isn't interested."

"Hey, anybody know the difference between an obnoxious drunken attorney and an obnoxious drunken regular person?" someone asked.

"What?" Casey asked, clearly trying to concentrate.

"When the regular person sobers up, he's not obnoxious anymore!"

"Obnoxious?" Casey asked. "Who's obnoxious? I'm just trying to give the lady a sample of my sterling Irish charm." He leaned in, tilting his face toward Erica's. "How about it? Can you appreciate my sterling Irish charm?"

"I'm fresh out of appreciation," Erica said, pushing past him. "If you'll excuse me—"

Ridiculous! Erica fumed as she stomped her way back to the sleeping cars. *That's what it was, plain and simple. She must have had rocks in her head to have left a nice, comfy bed to end up fighting off drunken attorneys. She had a ticket every bit as valid as the one held by Eric Sean O'Leary and*

*she was going to demand her rights to her half of that bed!
Better one lawyer in shamrock boxer shorts than a carload
of lawyers who've been swilling green beer.*

Her resolve faltered briefly after she stole back into the
compartment and found Sean O'Leary sleeping soundly—
until she remembered the rude way he'd awakened her earlier.

She raised her hand, aiming it strategically at the backside
she knew was covered with shamrocks and leprechauns. It
landed with a resounding *thwack!*

Sean sprang awake, wild-eyed and alarmed. "Whatisit?"
The urgent question came out as a single word.

"Before we go any further, I want to know if you're married, or . . . involved?"

"Married?" Sean shook his head to clear it. "Involved?"
Despite his wooziness, the realization hit him with the swift-
ness of a lightning bolt: *she was nuts.*

"I want to claim half of this bed, but first I want some as-
surance that I'm not going to have some woman on my
doorstep with a baby in her arms and a toddler hugging her
ankles sobbing because I slept with her husband and broke
up her home." Frowning, she added hastily, "Not that I'm
planning on doing anything but sleep."

Too bad. She might be nuts, but she was also . . . appealing.
"Your concern for the sanctity of family is laudable," he said,
yawning and stretching. "But I haven't had a wife in years."

She frowned at that, as if to say she'd figured as much.
"Here's the way it's going to be," she said. "I get the outside
so I can get out of bed without having to crawl over you. The
metal door stays open so anyone would hear if I should need
to yell for help. I get under the sheet and one blanket. You get
on top of them with the other blanket."

"I don't have any social diseases."

"That's nice to know," she said. "But hygiene isn't my only concern. There'll be no...nonessential touching." *They were tempting fate enough already. She was feeling terribly alone, and even with the lights out and her eyes closed, she wasn't likely to forget how gorgeous he was.*

Sean tried not to laugh, but a snicker leaked out anyway.

"I'm serious," she said.

"That's what makes it so funny." The laughter he'd managed to keep in earlier wheezed out. He gulped in a lungful of air and cleared his throat to regain his composure. "Legally speaking, 'nonessential touching' is a broad and imprecise term, open to interpretation."

Her eyes narrowed. "Don't give me any legal mumbo jumbo. You know *precisely* what I mean."

"Yes, ma'am," he said, swallowing a chuckle. "I know." He knew he was in for a restless night. He'd never expected her to accept his invitation.

If she knew how long it had been since he'd shared a bed with a woman, she'd probably run screaming from the compartment.

He hopped out of bed, straightened the bedding, folded back the top blanket and climbed back in. "Do I get a smiley-face sticker following instructions properly?"

"I don't give out stickers," she said tartly. "I use Happy Bugs rubber stamps."

Happy Bugs? "You're making that up," he said, segueing into a yawn.

"No. There's Buzzy the Busy Bee, and Hoppy the Happy Grasshopper, and—"

Busy Bees? Happy Grasshoppers? It was almost three o'clock in the morning, by God. "Can we turn out the light now so I can get back to sleep?" he said grumpily.

"Obviously you won't be getting any Happy Hoppys for attitude," she grumbled back from inside the nightgown she was using as a changing tent.

A moment later, the overhead fixture clicked off, leaving only the moonlike illumination of the night-light. Sean watched his new bunkmate wriggle to shake the full skirt of the long garment straight and wondered how he was going to get through the night without deciding that touching her was absolutely essential.

Turning to the bed, she gingerly lifted the bedding. The sleeves of the gown ended in ruffles that made her hands appear small and fragile.

A woman's hands. He closed his eyes against the sight, but it was too late; involuntarily, his mind made the link between gentle hands and loving touches. A familiar sadness swelled in his chest. *Gentle hands. Loving touches.*

Contrary to all the psychobabble hype about how men avoided commitment, some men were not meant to be solitary creatures. He wasn't. He missed having a woman in his life, missed a woman's gentle hands and loving touches. He missed passionate caresses and urgent groping in a darkened room.

She stretched out beside him, rigid with tension. The layers of fabric between them couldn't shield him from the solidity and warmth of her body. Nor were a sheet, a blanket and a sheep-festooned flannel gown a barrier to the scent of her hair. Strange how a man forgot the little things—like the way the scent of a woman's hair went straight to a man's senses and heated his blood.

It was going to be a very long night, he decided.

IT WAS GOING TO BE a very long night, Erica thought as she lay on her side, perilously close to the edge of the bed. As much as she needed sleep, she couldn't help wondering if she might have been wiser to stay in the lounge car. Suddenly, one good-looking Irish attorney in a narrow bunk seemed a lot more dangerous than a carload of fully dressed drunks—especially one wearing expensive after-shave.

After perhaps a minute and a half, her arm was hurting from having the bulk of her weight on it. She shifted slightly, undulating like an inchworm, trying to get comfortable while avoiding touching him.

Attempting to accommodate her, Sean pressed against the wall until the handle on the window cut into his back. His arms were crossed in front of him, and his left hand was in front of his face. Frowning, he wiggled his fingers, feeling like a vampire whose casket had been tipped on its side.

This was utterly ridiculous! Neither of them was going to get any sleep this way. "Don't get alarmed," he said. "I'm going to put my arm around you."

"No touching," she responded. "We agreed."

"We agreed on no *nonessential* touching," he argued. "But I have a window handle cutting into my back and you're about to fall off the bed. If I put my top arm across your waist, we'll both have a chance of getting some sleep."

He sensed her deliberation. "If I was trying to take advantage, I would have just grabbed you instead of telling you before I moved," he said.

She deliberated a bit longer before saying, finally, "Okay."

"Your enthusiasm is overwhelming," he grumbled as he scooted away from the window and draped his arm over her waist. It was good not having his hand in his face anymore. "You could move back just a bit," he suggested.

To his surprise, she did. Gradually, as she relaxed, her shoulders came to rest against his chest. The backs of her thighs aligned with the fronts of his, and her bottom nestled—

He couldn't prevent his body's physical reaction to having her pressed against him so intimately. "You may notice—"

"I already have."

"I can't do anything to . . . it's just a normal reaction." He let out a sigh of frustration. "What I'm trying to say is that you don't have to be alarmed."

"I wasn't," she said. *Self-conscious, maybe, and a bit embarrassed. But not alarmed.* "But thank you anyway for reassuring me."

He felt her body move as she breathed. Her hair was silky against his cheek. *How long had it been since he'd held a woman this way?* he wondered. *Just held her, without having had sex with her and with no expectations of it?*

Three years? Three years, two months and . . . how many days? His mind searched for the date and computed. Seventeen. Three years. Two months. Seventeen days.

Not that he was counting.

"You're not cold, are you?" she whispered.

"Cold?"

"I took most of the covers."

"Trust me," he said drolly. "I'm not cold."

"Men are always warmer than women," Erica murmured. Wonderfully warm. Gloriously warm. Somewhere near sleep, she sighed, snuggled closer to the stranger holding her and wondered if she was losing her mind. She didn't know this man, or anything about him, except his name and occupation. And his being an attorney certainly didn't win him any favor with her. But his warmth comforted, his strength reassured, and there had been few times in her life when she'd needed human warmth and reassurance more than she needed them tonight.

So she cuddled into the warmth and accepted the reassurance his presence offered. Tomorrow she would have to be strong for her grandmother; tonight she had this stranger's strength to draw on. Protected by the arm that circled her waist, she allowed herself, at last, to acknowledge the emotions she'd been denying since learning of her grandmother's illness. Fear and despair overwhelmed her. Her grandmother was dying. *Oh, God, what was she going to do? How was she going to endure it—the hospital, with its antiseptic smell and impersonal efficiency? Her grandmother, ill, suffering and growing weaker. How was she supposed to watch her grandmother die? And what was she going to do when her grandmother was gone?*

Her sorrow was too profound for hysterics or sobs. Except for a soft snuffle, she made no sound as tears spilled from her eyes and flowed over her cheeks.

"Is there anything I can do to help?" Sean's whispered words skittered through her hair.

"There's nothing anyone can do," she answered.

Sean tightened his arm around her and, cradling her face in his hand, wiped the moisture from her cheeks with his thumb.

A woman's tears. Acid on a man's heart. What was troubling her? he wondered. *Where had these tears come from?*

"I don't know your name," he said.

She pressed her cheek into the curve of his palm and put her arm over his, anchoring it close, cushioning his forearm between her breasts. "It doesn't matter." Eventually he felt the tension seep from her body as her breathing slowed. It had been a long time since a woman had aroused his protective instincts so fiercely. In fact, it had been a long time since a woman had aroused all his basic instincts so thoroughly.

Three years, two months and seventeen days, to be precise.

Not that he was counting.

3

STILL HALF-ASLEEP, Erica lay in the narrow bed of the compartment as wakefulness brought with it memories of where she was, why she was on the train and what had gone on the night before.

Sean O'Leary was gone, but as she rolled over, the faint scent of expensive after-shave bore witness to the fact that she had not dreamed the whole episode. She pushed up the window cover to let in the morning light and sat up, dropping her legs off the bed, wondering where her phantom bedmate had disappeared to.

Her eyes fell on a small rectangle of white paper that had been shoved under the knob that released the sink from the wall. He'd scrawled a note on the back of a business card:

The room is yours for the rest of the trip.

E. Sean O'Leary

Erica held the note a moment, vacillating between relief that she did not have to face him by light of day and regret that she had been denied the opportunity to thank him for his ... *what? Empathy? Understanding?* Maybe Sean's way was the best. She wouldn't have known what to say to him if he was here. She dropped the note into the trash receptacle, silently thanking him for sparing them both the embarrassment of a morning-after confrontation.

She washed and dressed, then put away the bed and slid the window screen up as she settled in the seat. From the hallway, she heard the car attendant announcing Washington, D.C., and knocking on the doors of those passengers who would be getting off there. The capitol dome glistened in the late-morning sunshine as they came into the city, a sparkling gold crown among towering white monuments and imposing buildings. A few minutes later, the train's whistle signaled their approach to the station.

Passengers in power suits and crisply tailored office attire crowded the platform, talking on cellular phones and constantly checking watches as they waited to board, clearly impatient to conduct official business on behalf of their respective companies.

Erica debated whether to try to get something to eat on the last hour of the ride, but decided against it out of fear of running into Sean O'Leary in the lounge car. In the brightness of the midday sun, she found it difficult to believe that the previous evening was not a figment of her imagination. She, Erica O'Leary, third-grade schoolteacher, could not have shared a bed with a man she'd met only once. It wasn't possible.

But it was. It had to be. The idea was too absurd for her to have imagined—and the memory was too real to deny. She remembered the way their bodies, chastely separated by the bedding, had spooned together. The way his body had warmed and hardened in response to being near hers. The strength and firmness of his arm between her breasts. The gentle touch of his fingers on her face and hair.

Who'd have believed a lawyer would turn out to be so sensitive and caring? If things had been different—

But things *weren't* different. Things were . . . the way they were. Each revolution of the wheels carried her closer to Baltimore and her terminally ill grandmother. She would probably never see Sean O'Leary again.

Impulsively, she fished the note he'd left her out of the trash, turned it over and ran the tip of her forefinger over the raised black ink spelling out his name, office address and phone number. *E. Sean O'Leary. Attorney-at-Law*. Maybe when her mind was clearer, she would think of something appropriate to say, and write him a note. She tucked the card into her purse. *Just in case*.

The reason for her trip pressed upon her with growing immediacy as the train drew closer to Baltimore, pushing Sean O'Leary, and her attraction to him, into relative insignificance. The whistle that had always triggered excitement over a journey's end sounded forlorn as a death knell as the train slowed. Erica waited until the last possible moment to leave the train, giving Sean O'Leary time to get out of the station. Then, dazed by dread, she hailed a cab and told the driver to take her to Johns Hopkins Hospital.

The drive passed in a blur. Erica entered the imposing building and asked directions to her grandmother's room at the front desk. Then, she fairly ran to the room, certain that she would forever remember the squeak of the wheels on her suitcase as she pulled it down that series of long halls. Upon reaching the room, she paused to catch her breath before entering, not knowing what to expect and afraid of what she'd find.

Her grandmother looked frail, but her bed was cranked up and she was awake and fully alert. "Gram?" Erica said, feeling helpless as a frightened child.

Her grandmother's blue eyes lit up. "Erica. I'm so glad you're here."

She held out her hands and Erica took them, squeezing gently, before spontaneously throwing her arms around her grandmother and hugging her tightly.

"Did you have an easy trip?" Gram asked, as if everything were perfectly normal.

Erica nodded. "I was able to get a sleeper." *And a compassionate human being who held me while I cried for you.*

"Good," Gram said spritely. "Then you're rested. That's good, because we don't have a lot of time. The doctor will be here soon. I've arranged for a private ambulance to take us to the house as soon as the paperwork's done."

"You're going home?" *Had it been a false alarm? Oh, God—let it have been a false alarm.*

"They've done everything they can do for me here," Gram said. "I've talked it over with the doctor and he agrees. There's nothing more anyone can do except make me comfortable, and I'd be more comfortable at home than in this smelly old hospital."

"Gram—"

Her grandmother closed her eyes and sighed, clearly drained by the brief exchange. Then, opening them again, she gripped Erica's hand tightly. "I know this is asking a lot of you, but I want to go home. I want to die in my own bed instead of in this mechanical marvel. It's like something out of a horror movie, grinding up, grinding down."

"Whatever you want, Gram," Erica said, wondering how she'd cope. But, as usual, her grandmother had thought of everything.

"I'll have a private nurse around the clock, so you won't be alone when it happens."

Erica nodded slowly. *Why had she thought her grandmother would be any different just because she was dying?*

FOR THE NEXT TWO DAYS, her grandmother remained conscious and alert, despite her waning strength. She insisted on keeping the curtains open and the blinds raised so that she could see the yard and watch the squirrels and birds frolic in the winter-bare trees. Erica read to her and talked to her in Gram's steadily shrinking moments of wakefulness. Then, on the third day after she'd returned home, Gram took Erica's hand in a grip that was urgent despite its weakness and said, "Don't worry about me, Erica. I'm finally going to see your mother again." A beatific smile spread over her face. "She's going to be so proud when I tell her what a lovely person you've become."

Her weak exhalation could hardly be called a sigh. "I'm tired now. Give me a kiss so I can rest a while."

Erica did as she was asked, knowing in her heart that Gram would never wake up again, and suspecting that Gram knew the same thing.

Her grandmother slid peacefully off to sleep.

MARIAN STONEHOUSE was dead.

Sean propped his elbows on his desk, buried his face in his hands and emptied his lungs in a prolonged sigh. It couldn't have happened at a worse time. Of course, there was no good time for a nice person to die. But it would have been easier to handle her death when he wasn't dealing with Judge Finkbein at the same time. The man had ice water in his veins; getting the magistrate to recess for the afternoon so that he could attend the memorial service had been like pulling teeth. Without anesthetic.

"Here's the file you asked for."

"Thanks, Roz," Sean said, looking up as he took the folder from his secretary.

"It's too bad about Mrs. Stonehouse. She was always so friendly."

"She was a special woman," Sean agreed, then paused pensively. "Did you take care of the flowers?"

Roz nodded. "A spray of coral roses. She wore coral a lot."

"Good choice," Sean said. "Thank you."

"What time is the memorial service?"

"Two o'clock," Sean replied. "I'll be leaving as soon as I go through a few things in this file."

"Give the family my condolences," Roz said.

"I will," Sean said. "But there's only a granddaughter. Mrs. Stonehouse outlived all her other close relatives."

"That's sad," Roz said. "She didn't seem that old."

She wasn't that old, Sean thought as he reviewed the contents of the folder. Seventy-eight. Her first husband died young, her only child had been killed in an automobile accident and her second husband, over twenty years her senior, died in his late seventies.

Locating the envelope he'd been looking for, he stared at it a moment, thinking how typical of Marian Stonehouse the mauve linen paper was. She must have known she was dying when she'd given him the letter to her granddaughter, but she'd said nothing. That, too, was like Marian Stonehouse.

He drove to the funeral home, steeling himself for the emotional ordeal. Memorials were still not easy for him, and this was more than a duty appearance. He'd been genuinely fond of his deceased client.

The funeral home was tastefully decorated, but it still smelled and sounded like a place of death. The cloying scent of cut flowers hung in the overcooled air and organ music emanated from the sound system to ineffectively mask the hollow, hushed silence. Sean located a pedestal sign bearing Marian Stonehouse's name beside the door of one of the home's three chapels, signed the guest register and entered the room. Inside, the less garish strains of a brass quartet replaced the organ music.

Sean's blood ran cold as his gaze settled on the closed coffin blanketed by ivy and small spring flowers and flanked by floral sprays and pedestaled arrangements. The polished wood casket and flowers with their mocking brightness were too similar to another such scene, and for a moment, he was transported back in time to a different chapel. *It shouldn't be this difficult. Everyone had told him time would make things easier, but the pain which had been festering for three years was as piercing as it had been on that horrible day.*

He forced himself to focus on the life-size color portrait of Marian Stonehouse displayed on an easel in front of the small pulpit, reminding himself that his purpose for being here today was to honor Marian's life and mark her passing. Having settled that issue in his mind, he decided to seek out Marian's granddaughter to offer his condolences.

Several people were clustered in the back corner of the room, speaking in hushed tones. Sean approached them, hoping to find Marian's granddaughter. He had no trouble picking her out, watching as she shook hands and thanked each guest for coming. But it was difficult to believe that the young woman greeting the mourners was the very woman who'd been in his thoughts almost constantly since he'd left the bed they'd shared together.

He would have recognized her anywhere—the strawberry blond hair, the pretty face, her slight frame. He'd hoped against futile probability that, somehow, he'd find her again, but he hadn't expected to find her at Marian Stonehouse's memorial service. She hadn't told him her name, and it had never occurred to him she might be Marian's granddaughter.

Erica Susan O'Leary. Everything clicked suddenly: she probably *had* had a ticket to the sleeper. She'd been coming to Baltimore to hold her dying grandmother's hand. And he'd tried to kick her out before offering her the option to share the bed with a total stranger who'd tried to pick her up in the lounge car an hour earlier! *Way to go, O'Leary. You win the worm-of-the-week award.*

She spotted him, and her face, already strained with emotion, registered shock, then annoyance as he worked his way toward her. Finally, they were face-to-face. Sean held out his hand, but she made no effort to accept it.

Her eyes narrowed. "I don't know how you found me," she said, her voice taut, "but your showing up here, at this time, is in extremely poor taste."

"I'm as surprised as you are," Sean said. "I didn't come here expecting to see you." *He'd left his card in the sleeper, hoping he would hear from her.* "I didn't know you were Marian's granddaughter."

"Marian?" she echoed, dumbfounded. "You knew my grandmother?"

"I was your grandmother's attorney."

The little color left in her face drained away, and for a horrible moment, Sean braced to catch her, fearing she might faint. But she didn't. She swallowed, then said, "I see."

"If I had known your name—"

She nodded gently, and he was relieved to note the color returning to her face. "I knew she had a new attorney after Mr. Reese died. She never mentioned your name."

"Your name," he corrected. "Almost. That's how she picked me out of the telephone directory."

A bittersweet smile brightened her face briefly. "That sounds like Gram."

"Yes," Sean agreed, allowing himself a grin. After an awkward pause, he said, "I didn't know your grandmother long— just over a year—but I liked her a great deal. It's hard to believe she's gone. She was always so full of life."

"Yes," Erica agreed with a noticeable quiver in her voice, "she was."

Another awkward silence ensued, lasting until two women entered the chapel and began walking toward them. Sean choked back emotion. "I'm sorry about your grandmother, Erica."

She thrust her chin up, struggling for composure. "Thank you. And . . . thank you for coming to the service. I'm sure Gram would have wanted you here."

The women were drawing near. It was time to move aside so Erica could greet them, but Sean was loath to leave her. She seemed vulnerable, just as she had in the train. Looking into her eyes as she struggled to rein in her emotions, he recalled the heat of her tears sliding onto his hand, the wetness of them on his thumb.

He hadn't gone a single waking hour without thinking of her since he'd climbed out of the sleeper.

Touching her elbow, he said, "I'll be nearby if you need me."

Erica nodded, then watched him walk away. *Her grandmother's lawyer.* She tried to absorb the significance of it, but she couldn't concentrate. Not here. Not now. She couldn't concentrate on anything when Gram—

She didn't have time to dwell on it. The women who'd just approached her introduced themselves as members of her grandmother's garden club and expressed their sympathy. As she shook their hands and thanked them for their kind comments, the funeral director stepped to her side. "Father Ryan is ready to start the service, Miss O'Leary. If you'll allow me to seat you . . ."

She numbly let him escort her to the front pew, feeling isolated and abandoned in the midst of the people who'd gathered to pay their respects to her grandmother. Their condolences, though comforting, couldn't fill the emptiness created by her grandmother's absence. Feeling less substantial than an oval of liquid from a children's bubble wand, she drew in a deep breath and released it slowly, hoping no one could tell how close she was to shattering.

Several pews behind her, Sean found it impossible not to stare at Erica. After days of thinking about her, hoping he could find her, he'd found her in the most unexpected place—and under the most unfortunate circumstances. A memorial service was not conducive to getting acquainted with a woman. And since she was Marian's granddaughter, technically, she was now his client.

She was dwarfed by the long, heavy pew on which she was seated. Her narrow shoulders were barely visible above the back. Her hair, drawn back sleekly and twisted into a knot just above her nape, evoked the memory of its sweet scent and silken texture. He'd burrowed his face in those soft strands as she slept. He recalled with haunting vividness the way she'd snuggled close to him in the narrow bunk, pressing her tear-dampened cheek to the back of his hand.

They had shared more that night than a narrow bed and body heat. They'd experienced something rare, intangible and elusive—an instinctive, human link that was sexual only in that they were of different sexes. Without knowing its source, he had recognized the desperate helplessness of grief in her. She'd needed comfort, and he'd comforted her. And what they'd shared was more intimate and binding than making love would have been.

She was alone. The fact registered abruptly. Someone should be with her. He concentrated, trying to remember what Marian had told him about her family. Her mother, Marian's daughter, had died when Erica was an infant, and her father had been in a feud with Marian ever since. There had been a couple of stepmothers, and numerous stepsiblings, all of whom had gone with their mothers following each divorce.

She had no family to comfort her. He'd just drawn the ugly conclusion when he saw the tremor pass through her shoulders. In a second he was on his feet, moving as unobtrusively as possible to the front pew. Her face registered surprise as he sat down beside her, giving her a small reassuring smile. "You look like you could use a friend."

"This is so difficult," she replied, focusing on the portrait of her grandmother. "It doesn't seem real, but it hurts—" Her features showed the strain of control as she swallowed.

"I know," he said. Far too well. He knew what it was to sit in a chapel, not believing what seemed impossible and hurting because, eventually, you have no choice but to accept the impossible as truth. Three years and almost three months.

In three years and almost three months, a person could suffer an eternity's worth of pain.

Her hands were in her lap, shredding the tissue she was holding. White flecks dotted the skirt of her black dress. Sean reached over, wrapped his hand around both of hers and squeezed. Her eyes expressed gratitude for his support as she gave him a sideways glance.

At that moment, the music from the sound system ceased abruptly and a hush descended over the chapel. The priest stepped up to the pulpit with a rustle of starched robes, and Erica produced a small sound in the back of her throat that Sean perceived as a muffled sob. She sat through the service stoically, pale and motionless as a plaster figurine while the priest and several of Marian's friends eulogized her. Sean suspected that Erica was not even aware that she was gripping his hand tightly, but he was glad he'd had the good sense to follow the impulse to sit down with her.

Ardeth Maxwell, the final speaker, wore a navy suit with a pin-striped scarf artfully anchored by a gold circle pin. Sean surmised she was in her early sixties.

"It's impossible to think of Marian without recalling her devotion to life and living things," she began. "She was a nurturer in the fullest sense of the word. In fact, she and I met through the Towson Green Thumbs." A bittersweet smile softened the woman's features and brightened her blue eyes. "Over the years, she and I grew everything from African violets to catnip, and every tree and shrub known to grow in Baltimore, plus a few that weren't supposed to. There's not a Towson Green Thumb that doesn't have some tree, vine or rosebush that originally came from Marian's garden or greenhouse."

She paused, visibly affected by the emotion of her speech. "People always told Marian she should open a nursery, but she said living things aren't for selling, that living things are for sharing with people you care about." She swallowed. "The Green Thumbs would like to show their appreciation for the love Marian shared with us for almost thirty years by planting a tree in her honor. The tree comes from a seedling from Marian's yard and is now almost ten feet tall. It will be moved to the Towson town square and surrounded by Lost Daughter roses, the registered rose that Marian developed and named in honor of her only child. The official dedication of this tree will be held on Marian's birthday in August, and a plaque with an appropriate text will be unveiled then."

Erica's chin quivered as she nodded. A tree in memory of her grandmother.

In memory of. Until that moment, she had been denying the finality of her grandmother's death, hiding in the endless details of things that had to be done. Now, the mention of a memorial tree brought reality crashing down around her. Her grandmother was gone. Erica had wanted to keep her grief private, not vent it in front of her grandmother's friends, but the tears she'd been holding in check came rushing forth on the heels of a mighty sob.

Just when she feared she would break down entirely, she became aware of a strong, comforting arm around her. She turned and tucked her head against a chest. A warm chest.

A broad chest that absorbed the sob and sopped up tears. A hard chest reassuring in its solidity. She spilled her tears and then snuffled, determined to regain her composure. The arm around her loosened slightly and as she turned her head, she discovered a handkerchief an inch from her face. She took it gratefully.

Sean remained at her side until the end of the service, then walked with her to the limousine provided by the funeral home. "Will there be anyone at your house?"

She nodded. "Gram's friends are going to come over for a while." She hesitated, then offered, "You're welcome to drop by."

"Thank you for asking," he said, "but as long as I know you're not alone, I won't intrude."

Erica hadn't even realized he was holding her hands until he squeezed her fingers gently.

"Well," she said.

He drew a business card and pen from his inside coat pocket and scrawled a number on the back before pressing it into her hand. "This is my home phone number. My office number is on the front. If you need anything—"

Erica nodded jerkily and tucked the card into her purse. "Thank you."

He stepped aside to allow the driver to assist her into the limousine. Inside the sleek, black vehicle, Erica wiped her hands over her face and relished the silence. With no one watching, she allowed herself a moment of defenselessness, bowing her head and letting her shoulders slump as she released a heavy sigh. The rest of the afternoon loomed ahead of her, poetic miles to go before she slept. She didn't feel like playing hostess, greeting her grandmother's friends and accepting their condolences. What she really wanted was to curl into a tiny ball and grieve in private.

The tears she'd shed in the chapel had been cathartic, easing some of the physical strain of trying to present a strong facade, but the big surge of relief over having the service behind her failed to materialize. She felt more drained than relieved. She had been determined not to break down during the memorial, but hearing about the tree had hit too close to home—her grandmother's home, and the things her grandmother held dear. It was an impressive tribute, and so appropriate for her grandmother. Her tears had flowed as much from pride and appreciation as from sorrow.

And Sean O'Leary had been there to comfort her. Sean O'Leary, of all people! She'd never expected to see him again, much less learn that he was her grandmother's attorney. And she'd certainly never planned to end up crying against his chest in the chapel, in front of the priest and her grandmother's friends. But, she admitted to herself, she'd been damned glad to have him there when she needed someone to lean on. For that matter, she'd been grateful to have his arms around her on the train, too.

Attorney or no attorney, the man was a virtual knight in shining armor.

"SEAN." He was the last person she'd expected to find on her doorstep when she'd heard the doorbell. Actually, she'd thought it was probably Gary, who was driving up from Georgia for spring break.

"I hope you don't mind my dropping by. I know you'll be in my office the day after tomorrow, but there are some things—" He heaved a sigh, ran his fingers through his hair and smiled sheepishly. "That's not true. I did come to bring you something, but it's nothing that couldn't have waited. The truth is, I found myself with an hour before I had to be at the courthouse, and I wanted to see how you were doing. Yesterday must have been exhausting for you."

Erica found his earnestness endearing. For a man with his good looks, he seemed surprisingly ill at ease admitting that he'd come specifically to see her. Like a bashful suitor. Smiling, she said, "I was just about to go out back and read the paper. It's so nice this time of day. Why don't we both go."

She led him to a concrete-and-wrought-iron bench nestled in the curve of a semicircular alcove fashioned from flowering shrubs and rosebushes. The shrubs, just beginning to leaf out, were lush with the promise of spring. The bench was narrow; their arms and shoulders almost touched as they sat down side by side.

"It's peaceful here," Sean said, casually stretching his arm across the back of the bench.

Erica caught the faintest whiff of his after-shave blending with the fresh air. "Gram always came out here to 'sit a spell' when she wanted to relax," Erica said. "She used to read to me here when I was a child. *Alice in Wonderland. Peter Rabbit. Winnie the Pooh.*"

She paused pensively. "Sitting here, it's hard for me to believe she's gone. I keep expecting her to come walking out of the house with glasses of iced tea with fresh mint or mugs of cocoa with a dollop of whipped cream on top. Never marshmallows—Gram thought marshmallows were disgusting." She shook her head gently. "The things that stick in your memory."

"Some places do that to you," he said. "As though some part of the person is still there, and if you just concentrated hard enough, you could—" Embarrassed, he dropped the thought in midsentence and shifted positions.

An awkward silence ensued before he asked, "Your grandmother is being interred this afternoon?"

Erica nodded.

"I don't mean to pry. I know the interment is private—"

"If you'd like to be there—"

"No. That's not it. It's just . . . you shouldn't go to the cemetery alone," he said. "It's too . . . you should have someone with you."

It fell short of being a formal offer to go with her, but the willingness was implied. "A friend of mine is coming in from Georgia," Erica told him, letting him off the hook.

He nodded as though relieved to have the matter settled. "Good."

He'd given her the perfect opportunity to express her appreciation for the concern he'd shown for her at the memorial service. Erica took a deep breath and said his name tentatively.

He turned his face toward hers expectantly. It was a handsome face, but not a flawless one. Fine lines fanned from the outside edges of his eyes, suggesting an old sadness reflected in the depths of his eyes, something he'd endured and survived, but which still haunted him.

"I wanted to . . . thank you," she said. "For, well, for being there at the memorial service yesterday. And that night on the train, too."

He dismissed her gratitude with a shrug of his shoulders. "Contrary to popular belief, lawyers *are* human."

"I know. But you were more than human. You were . . . kind." She became pensive, and they sat in companionable silence several minutes before she added, "I . . . I've never really lost anyone close to me. I was too young when my mother died to remember what it was like. I didn't anticipate falling apart the way I did."

"You didn't fall apart."

"I did. Not just yesterday, but on the train." *And he'd been there both times.* She chewed her lower lip. "That night—I don't usually—"

He lifted an eyebrow. "Sleep with strange men?"

Erica gave him a look that was part smile, part frown. "You enjoyed saying that, didn't you?"

"Not nearly as much as I enjoyed spending the night with you."

"I had just found out that Gram was ill," Erica said. She released a sigh that left her shoulders drooping. "I didn't think I would ever see you again, much less—"

Devilish amusement tugged at the corners of his mouth. "I hope you're not planning on telling anyone that we slept together," he said. "It would be extremely awkward if word got around. Technically, you're a client, and my professional reputation—"

"Your reputation is safe with me, Counselor," she assured him, in the same wry tone he'd used. "I wouldn't want it to get around that I slept with a lawyer any more than you want anyone to find out you slept with a client."

Close to a minute passed in silence before he said, "Erica, you've got to believe that I had no idea that you were Marian's granddaughter."

"I knew you were an attorney, but not that you were Gram's attorney." Her forehead crinkled. "Do you realize the odds against our meeting that way?"

"It wasn't as big a coincidence as it seems. O'Leary is not that uncommon a name, and Baltimore wasn't a random destination for either of us. If you had accepted my invitation for a glass of wine, we'd have introduced ourselves and we would have laughed about the coincidence, but we wouldn't have found it in the least peculiar. If you'd just shown me your ticket, I would have put it all together." He cocked his head curiously. "Why didn't you show me your ticket?"

"When I saw your name, it was obvious what had happened," she replied. "When the agent typed in my name to see if there had been a cancellation and a sleeper reserved in my name, your reservation came up and he printed out a ticket. Neither of us noticed the 'a' missing on the end of Erica. I was too distracted to notice anything." She sighed dismally. "The room was yours all along. I honestly believed the room was mine, but when I saw your name and realized—" She frowned self-consciously, embarrassed to confess, "I decided to bluff."

Shaking his head in consternation, Sean chortled. "If you'd shown me your ticket, I would have known right away that you were Marian's granddaughter. And if you'd told me that Marian was ill, I would gladly have given you the room."

"*Now* you tell me!"

"Are you really sorry about the way things worked out?"

Erica sensed his anticipation as he waited for her reply. Knowing she owed him total honesty, she pondered the question carefully before answering. *She'd felt so scared…so alone. It had been so good to have strong arms around her and human warmth next to her.*

"No," she admitted in a soft rush of sound. "I'm not sorry."

Sean savored her admission a moment, then smiled. Mesmerized by the heat in his eyes, Erica held her breath. They were a hairsbreadth away from a kiss. Mere inches separated their faces. He would need only to curl his arm off the back of the bench to embrace her…

Erica knew that if she moved even a fraction of an inch in his direction, he would kiss her. But as much as she longed to, she dared not make that move. Everything between them was too volatile, and anything more between them would be too complicated. *He was her grandmother's attorney.*

She turned her face away from him abruptly. "Did you say you had something for me?"

Lifting his arm from the back of the bench and passing it over her head in a wide arc, he took an envelope from his inside coat pocket. "This was in your grandmother's file, to be given to you in the event of her death."

Erica accepted the letter, handling it as though it might crumble into ashes at her touch. Her grandmother's stationery, her grandmother's handwriting.

"You'll want some privacy when you read it," Sean said. "I'll explore the yard a bit." He walked the perimeter of the lawn, paying scarce attention to the artful landscaping. He was too preoccupied thinking about Erica O'Leary. If she hadn't drawn back at the crucial moment—

But she had—leaving him hanging, wondering why. If she had been oblivious to the chemistry between them, he could have accepted that. But she had been as aware of it as he was. He was sure of it. *She was probably just as intimidated by the intensity of it as he was—and that was plenty intimidated.*

He waited a discreet interval, then returned to the alcove. Erica had finished reading the letter and was sitting with it open in her lap. He gestured to the empty side of the bench. "May I?"

"Of course," she said, unnecessarily smoothing her skirt onto her side of the seat.

"Are you all right?" he asked.

Smiling sheepishly, she rested her hand lightly on the letter. "My grandmother says I should trust you."

"That's what the letter was all about?"

Erica nodded. "She said that she knew I wasn't comfortable with lawyers, and she understood how I felt, because it wasn't easy for her to trust a stranger after Mr. Reese died. But she said she had come to trust you and felt I should, too."

"Do you?"

She sighed thoughtfully. "I'm not sure I have much choice. You're her attorney, and I—"

"If you want to move your legal business—"

"No," she said. "That's not what I meant. I—" She paused to collect her thoughts. "The truth is, I don't like having to deal with any lawyer about anything."

"I'll try to be gentle," he said drolly.

"You've given me more cause to trust you than to distrust you," she said. She turned her face toward his. "I think I'm angry that grandmother died, and I'm trying to find someone to blame. Does that make any sense?"

"It makes perfect sense," Sean replied. "Anger is a normal phase of grief, just like denial."

"You seem to know a lot about grief."

"Contrary to popular belief, lawyers—"

"Are human?" she asked, cocking an eyebrow.

"Lawyers grieve like everybody else," he completed soberly. "And I deal with a substantial number of clients who are going through the grief process."

"Are we—ethically speaking—are we allowed to discuss my grandmother's estate?" Erica asked after a pensive pause. "Informally?"

"What do you want to discuss?"

She hesitated. "Was my grandmother in debt?"

Sean's face registered genuine surprise. "What makes you ask that?"

"Something in her letter. She said that I was going to need a lot of help and that she regretted not preparing me better, but she didn't want anything to strain our relationship when she was alive. I've been trying to think what she would have to prepare me for, and debt is the only thing I came up with."

"Your grandmother was not in debt," he said. "Her estate is complicated, but I can put your mind at ease about that right off the top."

"I don't understand why it would be compli . . ." Her voice trailed off as she tilted her head toward the front of the house, listening. "Did you hear a car stop out front?"

"Are you expecting anyone?"

"My friend from Georgia. That could be him. I'd better check." She jumped up and walked around to the side of the house where she could see the driveway.

Him? It hadn't occurred to Sean that there might be a *him* in her life, that her friend from Georgia might be a *male* friend.

"It is him," she told Sean. Waving broadly, she called out, "Gary! Around here!"

Sean clenched his teeth and tried not to notice the sunlight glinting in Erica's strawberry blond hair as he waited curiously for the mysterious Gary to come into view. He was as anxious to see him as Erica apparently was—for totally different reasons. If this Gary was more than a friend to her . . .

Gary turned out to be a boy-next-door, Eagle Scout kind of guy, wearing a pair of worn corduroy jeans, a V-necked sweater and a cotton shirt open at the neck. Sean would have put him in front of any jury in the country with confidence that no one would doubt his word, but he experienced a disconcerting stab of animosity toward him as the man pulled Erica into an enthusiastic bear hug.

"How was your trip?" Erica asked, stepping out of his embrace.

"Long," Gary replied.

"You didn't have to throw away your spring break to come hold my hand," Erica said.

Sean instantly disliked the familiarity implicit in Gary's boyish grin. "I didn't come to hold your hand. You know how I am about history—I came to freeload in your guest room and take in our nation's capital while I'm in the general vicinity."

He noticed Sean at the same time Erica seemed to remember that he was there. "Gary, this is Sean O'Leary, attorney-at-law."

"O'Leary?" Gary asked, surprised.

"Isn't that a hoot?" Erica said. "His first name is Eric. My grandmother chose him because his name is so similar to mine. Sean, this is Gary Wisdom, the vice principal at the school where I teach, and a very dear friend. He drove up from Georgia to comfort me—and see the Smithsonian."

"And the FBI headquarters," Gary replied affably, shaking Sean's hand. "It's nice to meet you, Mr. O'Leary."

"I'm sure your being here will mean a great deal to Erica," Sean said. "I was concerned about her being alone here."

Obviously, he need not have worried.

4

"NICE SUIT," Gary said, gesturing toward the outfit she held in her hands.

"Maybe it'll give me some confidence when I go to Sean's office tomorrow," Erica said. They were waiting in line at the cashier's stand in a department store that sold high-quality clothing at a discount. "I don't know why, but Sean says it's going to be complicated."

"So what's up between you and the good attorney?" Gary asked.

"My grandmother's estate," Erica said.

"And that's why you're buying a sexy new suit? Sorry, but that story doesn't wash."

"I'm buying a suit because I've been needing one for a long time. This one fits, and it's marked down far enough to suit a schoolteacher's budget."

"And it's sexy."

"Sexy?" Erica said. "It's not sexy."

"I don't know much about women's clothes, but I know when something is sexy," Gary insisted. "It has all that lace at the . . . on the—you know." He gestured self-consciously toward his chest. "Up front."

Erica laughed. "You're blushing, Gary."

"At least I made you smile."

"You were right about getting out of the house," she said. "It has been good to get away." Between the memorial service and her anticipation of seeing Sean again, she'd been overwhelmed without even realizing it.

"I just told you that so I'd have a private tour guide," Gary said. She'd taken him on a walking tour of downtown Baltimore, pointing out landmarks and monuments, then they'd eaten crab cakes for lunch at the Inner Harbor. Erica had spied the huge sale banner outside the department store as they were driving back to her grandmother's house. "And I think you're trying to impress him."

"Who?"

"Mr. Eric Sean O'Leary. Who else?"

"Maybe a little," she admitted.

"A little?"

"Okay," Erica confessed. "A lot. I want to make him sit up and take notice when I walk into his office."

"You could walk into his office wearing baggy sweats and he would sit up and take notice," Gary said.

Erica's eyes narrowed with a skepticism that matched the irony in her voice as she said, "Right."

"Are you being coy, or are you truly oblivious?"

"I must be oblivious. I don't know what you're talking about." *Liar!*

"I think you do," Gary said. "No woman is *that* oblivious to a man's interest."

Erica heaved a sigh. "It's so . . . *pointless.*"

"Pointless? Why? He's definitely interested—he's not married, is he?"

Erica shook her head. "No."

"So where's the problem?"

"He's a lawyer," she said, frowning. "And not *just* a lawyer. He was Gram's lawyer, which makes him my lawyer, which means absolutely nothing could ever come of it."

"That's pure bunk and you know it," Gary said. "Attorneys socialize with clients. The man likes you. A lot."

They moved forward a few steps in line. "What gives you that idea?"

"Male intuition."

"I didn't know there was such a thing."

"That's because you don't have any testosterone," Gary said.

"A deficiency I can live with," Erica quipped.

"Well, if you had any, you'd have picked up on the fact that your lawyer friend didn't like me."

"That's preposterous. He barely met you, and he was perfectly polite."

"Well, despite the fact that he managed to be polite, he didn't like me. And since I'm an altogether likable fellow, and I'm not nearly as good-looking as he is, and I probably don't make a quarter of what he makes in a year, we must assume that the source of his animosity arose from the one area in which I was a threat to him—you."

"You've just proved it," she said, slapping her suit on the counter to have the tags scanned.

"Proved what?"

"My theory that testosterone converts human brain tissue into rocks." She gave the cashier her credit card.

"Well, I have a theory, too," he said.

"I'm afraid to ask."

"I'll tell you, anyway," he said, tossing his six-pack of sports socks on the counter as the cashier bagged Erica's suit. "The theory is that when a woman knows she's wrong about something, she starts insulting the man she's arguing with."

SEAN'S OFFICE was located in a cottagelike complex housing a dozen office suites, but despite the cozy ambience, it *was* a law office, Erica thought anxiously. The receptionist paused in the process of watering a hanging basket of angelwing begonias to greet Erica. "You must be Erica O'Leary. I'm sorry about your grandmother. She was a sweet lady. I'll let Mr. O'Leary know that you're here."

"Mr. O'Leary knows," came Sean's voice from the hallway. He emerged from the doorway and smiled at Erica. "Come on back. Would you like some coffee?"

"No, thank you," Erica said. She was edgy enough without caffeine.

In keeping with the cottagey atmosphere, Sean's office was decorated in warm colors and relaxed lines. The tweed-upholstered overstuffed sofa and chairs in the conversation area, were plump and inviting, and the wood-and-leather chair on the client's side of the desk was well-padded on the seat and arms. Sean indicated that Erica should sit there as he walked to the executive armchair behind the desk.

"Are you up to this?" he asked solicitously.

Erica nodded. *Did it matter? Ready or not, she had to face it.*

"We have a lot to go over, but I'll make this as easy as I can," he said, his manner turning crisply professional.

Erica's stomach tied in knots. She'd been in and out of law offices since she was eye level with the glass apothecary jars of hard candies so many of the receptionists had kept on their desks, and she'd heard that tone of voice too many times not to recognize an attorney in action. Despite his informality—his suit coat was hanging on the coatrack and the sleeves of his dress shirt were rolled up—he was no longer the man who'd held her while she cried. He was an attorney.

"Before we go through your grandmother's will, I'll tell you that it is actually simple and straightforward."

"Simple? I thought you said it was complicated."

"The situation is complicated," he said. "The will itself is simple."

Situation? Erica wondered frantically. He was talking in lawyer gibberish.

"There are some miscellaneous bequests, but you are, essentially, her only heir."

"What kind of bequests?" Erica asked.

Sean's eyebrows lowered as he skimmed the document in front of him. "There's a grant to the Towson Green Thumbs Garden Club, an endowment of a scholarship to the university and a cash gift to your father."

Erica was astounded. "She left my father money? They fought like cats and dogs. My father wouldn't even come to the memorial service."

"Your mother was your grandmother's only child. Your grandmother was afraid that your father might try to make some claim on the estate by virtue of the fact that he was married to your mother at the time of her death. In order to head off that sort of grab, she left your father ten thousand dollars, with the stipulation that he agree never to pursue any claim against the remainder of the estate."

"None of this makes any sense," Erica said. "The remainder of the estate? Was she afraid he would want her house, or her car?"

"Although your grandmother chose to live simply, her estate is sizable."

"How...sizable?" Erica said, trying to assimilate the information.

"Aside from the physical property, which includes her house and car, your grandmother was holding an investment portfolio worth in the neighborhood of two million dollars."

"Two million dollars?" Erica wheezed.

"Give or take a few thousand dollars depending on the current market quotes."

It was incredible! "Where would Gram get two million dollars?"

"Marian anticipated your surprise."

"*Surprise* is too mild a word," Erica said.

Sean saw the color drain from her face and dashed to the watercooler to draw her a glass of water. He pressed the glass into her hand. "Here. Sip."

Her hair smelled like strawberries, just as it had on the train. He'd done a lot of thinking about that faint suggestion of strawberry.

She nodded jerkily and took a sip. Sean stepped back and leaned against the front of his desk and crossed his arms loosely over his waist, watching her drink the water. "You've got some color back in your cheeks," he observed finally. "Good. You were looking a little peaked."

"I was feeling a little peaked," she admitted.

"Perfectly normal under the circumstances," he assured her. He was used to seeing the heirs of his recently deceased clients under stress. Wills and estates were emotional business. He tried to be sensitive and understanding with his clients. Usually his concern was human and professional.

With Erica O'Leary, his concern was human and *personal*. He didn't want merely to be understanding, he wanted to comfort her. He didn't want merely to sympathize, he wanted to take away her sorrow. At the very least, he could make her more comfortable. "What do you say we blow this joint and find some fresh air and sunshine?" he suggested.

"Can we do that?"

"A woman with two million dollars can do just about anything she wants," he said. Ignoring her benign scowl, he continued, "Seriously, there's no reason for us to sit around in a stuffy old office on a beautiful spring day. I've given you the gist of the will. You'll have plenty of time to go over the actual text at your leisure."

Erica shrugged. "Why not?"

"I'll have Roz call a deli a few blocks away. We'll grab some sandwiches and have lunch outside somewhere."

The deli was strictly upscale. Their lunch came packed in a cardboard box printed to resemble a wicker basket. From the deli, they drove to the small park adjacent to the lawn of the Hampton Mansion. Although the road was less than a football field's length away and the mansion loomed within easy sighting distance, they were, for all practical purposes, as alone as they would have been on a proverbial desert island.

"Now, isn't this better than being inside a law office?" Sean asked as he removed a plastic table cover printed with the traditional red-and-white-checked design from the deli box and spread it over the picnic table.

"*Anywhere* is better than a law office," Erica replied.

Sean winced, then continued setting out the bright red plastic plates and cutlery.

"This is what you call 'grabbing some sandwiches'?" Erica challenged as he took out individual-serving bottles of blended juices and cartons of gourmet salads, artfully sliced fruits and vegetables, spreadable cheeses and petite muffins of several varieties.

"I'm introducing you to the style to which you may become accustomed," he said, smiling.

Erica returned the smile as they filled their plates. "If this crab salad is a sample of what an heiress eats, I'm hooked," she said after tasting it.

"That's the deli's specialty," Sean said. "Along with the zucchini muffins. Try one."

"You talked me into it," she said, picking up one of the muffins and biting off half. "Heaven," she announced, unconsciously running the tip of her tongue over her bottom lip before putting the second half in her mouth.

He'd never kissed her. They had been almost as close as two human beings could get, and still, he'd never kissed her. Sean felt that deprivation as he watched her lift the bottle of juice to her mouth.

"You're supposed to be telling me how my grandmother could have an investment portfolio worth two million dollars without anyone knowing it," she said after putting the bottle back on the table.

Sean nodded. His mind had been miles away. Forcing his thoughts back to the subject they'd come to discuss, he said, "Your grandfather left a generous life insurance policy when he died, and your grandmother wisely decided to invest it and live off the income it generated, rather than piecemealing the principal away. She lived very comfortably for a number of years—until your mother's death."

He paused to take a breath. "Within a short time, it became obvious that your father, with whom her relationship had always been tenuous at best, was disinclined to allow her access to you. Her efforts to secure the legal right to see you quickly became expensive."

"Not just in dollars," Erica said bitterly.

"No. Not just in dollars." The reflection of remembered pain in the depths of her eyes made him want to fold her in his arms and hug her until that deep-seated anguish subsided. "But your grandmother had already lost her husband and her only child. You were all she had left. And she was genuinely concerned for your welfare."

"If my father hadn't been so pigheaded—"

"Nevertheless, he was. From what your grandmother told me, the more determined she grew to maintain regular contact with you, the more determined he became to prevent it. Her financial adviser, Jason Stonehouse, became concerned when she began to break into her principal in order to keep the attorney on the case, and he was sympathetic to her plight. They were both widowed and lonely, and they established a close rapport that grew into a close friendship and, ultimately, marriage. It was largely a marriage of convenience. His generous income allowed her to continue her legal battle."

"I always understood that Gram and Jason had agreed before they married that Jason would leave his money to his children."

"Yes, they had a prenuptial agreement. All the assets he'd acquired prior to their marriage, including the insurance from his first wife and the income it had generated, were divided among his three children. However, Stonehouse himself was heavily insured, and your grandmother was beneficiary to half of his life insurance. As she had done before, she invested it and lived off the interest—or what she needed of the interest. And as fate would have it, she developed an excellent rapport with her late husband's partner."

"Mr. Reese."

Sean nodded. "Reese was much closer to your grandmother's age than Stonehouse had been. He had actually started at the firm as Stonehouse's protégé. He proved to have something of a Midas touch. Your grandmother's portfolio grew from generous to truly impressive under his supervision. And she and Mr. Reese became . . . *close*."

His odd inflection gave the statement innuendo. "Why did you say it that way?" Erica asked. "As though there was something—" She couldn't bring herself to say anything so absurd about her grandmother.

"There was," he said.

"I don't believe you," she said. She couldn't take that, on top of two million dollars. It was just too farfetched.

"Not at first," he said. "For the first two years he managed her account, their relationship was purely professional. Then Mrs. Reese suffered a massive stroke that left her comatose. When therapy proved nonproductive, she was put into a residential treatment center. Your grandmother comforted

Mr. Reese. Having gone through something similar, although not as prolonged, with Stonehouse, she understood what he was going through. They didn't start out with the expectation of becoming romantically involved, but two lonely people—"

"She and Mr. Reese were—"

"Intimately acquainted. Yes. They considered marriage after Mrs. Reese died, but they decided it would be too complicated. Both of them were settled in houses they were fond of, and both of them were financially independent. It worked out better for them to pursue their friendship while maintaining their individual households and holdings."

"Grandmother and Mr. Reese," Erica mused aloud. "I never even suspected."

"No one sees their parents as sexual beings. It would be doubly hard to think about a grandparent that way." *Not that he was having any trouble perceiving Marian Stonehouse's granddaughter as a desirable woman, especially when the corner of her mouth tipped down in a pouty frown.*

"I seem to have been oblivious to a lot of things where my grandmother was concerned," Erica said, adding abruptly, "I feel like taking a walk."

In order to leave the picnic table, she had to turn her body and lift her legs over the bench. Instead of getting up, though, she sat on the bench with her back to the table. "Damn!"

"What is it?"

"Just a run in my stocking."

But her voice said otherwise. Sean got up and walked around the table. She had crossed her left leg over her right and was examining the damage in the stockings that matched her peach-colored suit perfectly.

"Too bad," he said. "They look expensive." While he tried to focus on the ragged, half-inch-wide tear extending from her knee to her ankle on the inside of her calf, it was the shapely leg inside the torn stocking that captured his attention.

"They're worthless now," Erica said. Propping her elbows on her knees, she buried her face in her hands. Her shoulders vibrated with the force of a shuddering sigh.

"It's not just the run in your stocking," he said.

She lifted her head. "No," she agreed. "It's not just the run in my stocking. It's . . . everything."

"You're not going to need a hanky again, are you?"

"No," she said firmly. "I've already exceeded this month's tear quota."

"You're entitled to some tears. You just lost someone you loved."

She stared blankly at the ruined stocking. Seconds later, she spoke softly. "Do you know what hurts the worst?" She didn't wait for a response. "It's not only that she's gone. It's that I thought . . . when I got here and she was still alert, I thought we had been given a gift—the chance to say the things that people regret leaving unsaid. I was able to tell her that I loved her, and that I understood why she did the things that I didn't always understand, and apologize for not understanding sooner. I actually felt fortunate, and then—"

Despite her earlier resolve not to cry, tears welled in her eyes. "I thought we'd tied all the loose ends, and then, today—" She wiped her damp cheeks with her fingertips. "My grandmother's gone, and I'm finding out that I didn't know her at all."

Sean sat down next to her and stretched his arm across her shoulders. She turned into his embrace, resting her ear against the front of his shirt. "Gram shared the most intimate details of her life with you, things she didn't tell me."

"I was her attorney."

"Is that supposed to make me feel better—to learn that she confided in a *lawyer*, when she wouldn't confide in me?"

"People often tell their attorneys things they don't tell relatives. Sometimes it's a simple matter of conducting business."

"Her relationship with Mr. Reese wasn't business."

"She informed me of her personal relationship with Reese on her first visit," Sean said. "I was taking over executorship of her holdings, and she felt I had a right to know that their relationship had been more than professional. She considered it a question of ethics."

"That explains why she told you, but not why she didn't tell me."

"A woman her age and from her generation might well have considered withholding such information from a granddaughter a matter of discretion."

Erica digested the comment a moment before challenging, almost hostilely, "What about the money? Why would she keep a veritable fortune a secret? Not even a hint. I thought . . . she always lived so—"

"Simply," Sean said.

Erica nodded. "She always said she liked to keep things simple, but I never realized that it was more from choice than from necessity."

"She was happy in her house, puttering in her garden. That's the main reason she and Reese never married. She was too content right where she was."

"I can understand her choosing to live simply," Erica said. "But *so much* money! Not to tell me—prepare me, discuss it with me—seems like a deliberate deception by omission. That's so unlike Gram. Why the secrecy?"

"Your grandmother didn't want anything to jeopardize the relationship she'd fought so very hard to maintain through the years—especially not money."

"Did she think it would make a difference in the way I felt about her? Was she afraid that I would care more about the money than her? That I would put arsenic in her morning tea so I could inherit it sooner? Didn't she know me better than that?"

"Your grandmother wasn't afraid of how you would react. She was afraid of how your father and step-siblings would. She didn't want to risk putting you in an awkward situation with them if they knew, and she didn't want to burden you with having to keep a secret from them. That's why she left money to your father. She knew any kind of legal battle would be emotionally devastating for you, so she hoped to head off any grab attempt by—"

"She knew I wouldn't fight him, so she paid him off up front," Erica said.

"It was a shrewd maneuver on her part."

She lifted her gaze to his. "So, Counselor, what am I supposed to do now?"

Sean shrugged his shoulders and threw his hands in the air in a gesture of abandon. "Anything you'd like." He'd never seen a woman look quite so bewildered. Grinning, he said, "Surely you have some secret fantasy, something you've always said you'd do if you won the lottery."

"Have my front struts replaced?" she said dubiously.

"You can replace your entire car if you like," Sean said. "Quit your job, take a cruise around the world."

"Do they really have cruises that go around the world?"

Sean chuckled. "Yes."

"I'd be more likely to charter a bus and take my homeroom class to DisneyWorld." She sighed. "Guess I need to work on my sense of adventure a little."

"Give yourself some time. You've only known that you're wealthy for an hour." He leaned forward, poised to stand up. "How about that walk you were going to take? Mind some company?"

"I would love some company," Erica replied.

Side by side, they followed the road over the crest of the hill and down the other side.

"Gram's dogwood is blooming," Erica said. "It was her favorite tree." She paused pensively. "I noticed the first blossoms when I walked out to the limo to go to the memorial service. It was almost as though Gram were trying to say goodbye."

"Maybe she was," Sean said. Reaching the bottom, they turned around and started back up the rise.

Sean smiled reassuringly. "It sounds like you loved your grandmother very much."

She turned her head. "I can't believe anything that's happened. It's so...unreal. You always think, 'If I just had money, I'd—' but then, suddenly, you find out you do, and it doesn't seem real."

"Give yourself time. You don't have to make any major decisions right away."

"My mind is mush. Right now I couldn't make a decision about what to have for dinner."

"I could take you to dinner and order for you."

She smiled. "I was speaking rhetorically."

"The invitation stands."

Her smile waned. "Thanks, but there's enough food at Gram's house to feed a small army. If I can't decide what to eat, I'll just point at the foil-covered serving dishes and say eeny-meeny-miney-mo."

"I didn't invite you because I thought you'd go hungry."

"I know." She knew *exactly* why he'd invited her, and the prospect was daunting. Going to dinner with him wouldn't be a serendipitous encounter, nor would they be able to pretend it was anything other than what it was—a man taking a woman to dinner. For all the usual reasons. They wouldn't be able to hide behind their lawyer-client relationship. They would be a man and a woman on a date. "But it would be a shame to let all that food go to waste."

"I see," Sean said. *Clearly.* If she was really concerned about the food going to waste, she'd have invited him over to help eat it. The dark possibility that maybe someone else was dipping into those casserole dishes occurred to him. "Is your friend still here—the principal?"

"Vice principal," she corrected. "Gary took the train to D.C. this morning. He's probably browsing his way through the American History Museum as we speak. He won't be back until tonight. And no."

"No?"

"No, Gary and I aren't involved. He's just a very dear friend."

"You didn't tell me you read minds."

"Figuring out what you were really asking was a no-brainer," she said.

"What about back in Georgia?" he asked. "Is there anyone there counting the minutes until you return?"

She thought a moment. "There's Timothy Scott."

Sean swallowed his disappointment and, against his better judgment, asked, "Is it serious?"

"It is to Timothy. He's probably getting pretty anxious to see me by now. He's shy, so he hates having a substitute."

"Substitute?"

"Teacher," she said with a grin.

Sean frowned grumpily. "You had me going."

She acknowledged the statement with a nod. Her teasing mood evaporated in the silence that followed. Finally she drew a deep breath. "I'm not seeing anyone. But, Sean—"

"Don't try to deny that you don't feel the attraction between us."

"I feel it," she said, "but . . . I'm overwhelmed right now, and you're—"

"A lawyer?" he said bitterly.

"Not just a lawyer," she said. "*My* lawyer. I seem to have inherited you along with the millions." She took in a deep breath and released it slowly. "I've never seen you when I wasn't ... vulnerable, and you've been understanding and ... helpful. I want you to know that I appreciate that."

Sean grinned smugly. "Could it be that I've actually found a chink in that lawyer-hating armor you wear?"

She stopped walking abruptly to look him squarely in the eyes. "I'm still vulnerable, Sean. I seem to have a hard time remembering that you are a lawyer."

"I seem to be having a hard time remembering it myself," he said, pulling her into his arms.

She said his name as he lowered his mouth to hers, but he shushed her. "This is long overdue."

Not only overdue, but inevitable. It had been inevitable since the moment she'd walked into the lounge car on the train. Since he'd first stood next to her and discovered how small she was. Since he'd felt her body pressed against his and smelled her hair. Since her warm, wet tears had flowed over his hand as she nestled her cheek against it. Since he'd found her in the chapel after worrying that he'd never see her again.

She was soft and warm, gentle and responsive—all the things a woman should be. All the things his lonely soul hungered for. Ending the kiss taxed his willpower, but the effort was rewarded by the sight of her face, cheeks rouged and lips plumped by their kiss.

"Shouldn't you be getting back to your office now?" she asked.

"I'm not in any hurry," he said, and dipped his head to kiss her again.

5

"WHEN DO YOU HAVE to go back to Georgia?" Sean asked as he drove back to his office.

"We're leaving Saturday morning."

"We?" he asked curiously.

"I'm riding back with Gary. It'll save me the price of a train ticket, and he won't have to drive all that way alone."

"Of course," he growled. "I should have realized. Not that you need to save money."

Erica was still savoring the note of male jealousy she heard in his voice, when he asked, "What are you going to do about the house while you're away?"

"Ardeth Maxwell has some seedlings started in the greenhouse, so she's going to look after everything there, and Gram's neighbor, Mrs. Winkle, said she and her husband would keep an eye on the house for me. Their son is stationed overseas and left his car with them, so they're going to park it in Gram's driveway from time to time, and I'm going to put some lights on timers to make the house look lived in. And Gary's going to help me install some dead-bolt locks that can't be picked with a credit card."

"Good old Gary," Sean mumbled under his breath. At the next red light, he turned to look at her. "There's no tactful way to say this. You said yourself that you're vulnerable now, and—"

"I've already told you, Gary and I—"

"Not that. I wanted to caution you . . . I just wanted to suggest that you use discretion in telling anyone about your inheritance. You're an attractive woman, and the world is full of men who'd count that as a bonus while they're trying to get their hands on two million dollars."

"I've already told Gary," she said. "In confidence. I called him this afternoon. And yes, I trust him to keep it confidential."

He smiled briefly before turning his attention back to the traffic as the light turned green. "That habit you have of reading minds is nerve-racking."

"I wouldn't have told him if I hadn't known he would keep the information to himself," she said. "I'm not ready to deal with any hoopla over this yet."

"When will you be back?"

"As soon as school's out for the summer. Maybe I'll have a better idea what I want to do with the house by the time school starts again in the fall."

"Are you considering selling it?"

"I'm not sure I could stand to do that. I feel so close to Gram there."

They spent the rest of the short drive in silence. After parking the car outside his office, Sean twisted in his seat to face Erica and surprised her by reaching out to hold her hand. She was acutely aware of him as a man at that moment—his size, his warmth, the scent of his cologne, the strength and gentleness of his touch. The sensual memories of the kiss they'd shared were vivid and immediate. *Why?* she wondered. *Why this man? And why now, when her whole world had been turned topsy-turvy?*

"I feel responsible for you," he said.

"You ought to," she replied, aiming for a touch of levity. "You're in charge of my fortune."

"I'm not talking about Eric Sean O'Leary, attorney-at-law," he replied.

"I was afraid of that," she said.

"It's a difficult time for you," he said. "If there's anything I can do, personally or professionally—"

"You wouldn't want to look after a fat old house cat who's used to a lot of attention, would you? Gary's allergic to cats, so we can't take her back with us. Ardeth would feed her, but Esmerelda's used to a lot of petting, so I'd hate for her to be alone for very long."

"Sure, I'll keep her."

Erica couldn't believe he'd agreed to take the cat. "You will?"

"Sure. Why not? We used to have a cat. I wouldn't mind having one around again. I wouldn't mind having an excuse to see you again before you leave, either."

"She likes a lot of attention," Erica said dubiously.

"I'll make sure she gets petted and played with regularly. If I don't, you can sue me."

They exchanged grins.

"So when do I pick up the cat?" he asked.

"Saturday morning at eight o'clock?"

"I'll be there."

"EITHER YOU'RE EARLY, or I'm running late," Erica said.

"Good morning to you, too," Sean said, stepping into the entry hall. He consulted his watch. "I'm two minutes early. Does that ease the situation?"

"Not as much as two hours would," she said. She was wearing jeans and a loose-fitting chambray shirt with flowers embroidered on the yoke. The long sleeves were rolled up into soft cuffs at her elbows. She looked like a woman who would be perfectly comfortable sitting on the floor surrounded by children and toys.

Probably because she is a woman who would be comfortable sitting on the floor surrounded by children and toys, he thought. Given the way he was drawn to her, it was a thought both reassuring and disturbing.

"Busy?" he asked superfluously.

"I didn't realize how many details there would be," she said. "I've got the refrigerator cleaned out and turned off, but I can't reach around the back to unplug it."

Sean scanned the room. "Where's Super Principal?"

She responded with a scowl devoid of genuine malice. "He went to fill up the gas tank and put air in the tires. I'm supposed to be ready to go by the time he gets back, but I've still got a dozen things to do—"

"Calm down," he said, taking her upper arms in his hands. "You're in a complete tizzy."

Her face registered surprise before she gave a chortle of laughter. "A tizzy?"

"You know what a tizzy is, don't you?"

"It's what I'm in," she said. "It just wasn't an expression I would have expected you to use."

"I had a grandmother, too," he said. "Lawyers aren't spawned, you know."

"I was never really sure," she countered.

"I assure you, I'm one hundred percent human," he said, stepping close enough to slide his arms around her. "Otherwise, I wouldn't be succumbing to the irresistible urge to kiss you."

Erica had known he was going to kiss her from the moment he'd touched her. And she'd been waiting. Anticipating. Waiting to see how he would accomplish it. Anticipating the way his touch made her heart race, her blood move faster, her head feel light. Anticipating the mystery and magic and fascination of sexual compatibility, that strange chemistry that drew two people together in defiance of logic or conscious desire. It was ridiculous, really. They had nothing in common. He was a lawyer. Any personal relationship would be dangerous and absurd. And yet . . .

They might have kissed a thousand times before instead of just once. The memory of the comfort he'd offered her while they were still strangers linked her to him as forcefully as the sexual chemistry drawing them together. He had slept with her, comforted her; his arms were familiar, being in his embrace as natural as breathing.

"This is crazy," she said as his mouth moved toward hers.

"Insane," he agreed in a growl.

"Unwise," she said in a breathless whisper a second before his lips brushed hers. After that, there were no words. No damning adjectives for the folly they were engaging in. There was only the pleasure they shared, the splendor of sensation.

A soft sigh of yearning parted Erica's lips as his mouth brushed hers again. He immediately crushed her closer and deepened the kiss. The affinity was there instantly, the invisible bond that had been forged between them as they lay together in that narrow bed on the train. With the melding of their mouths, he seemed to absorb her pain and confusion, to endow her with his strength. Need and desire twisted into a vibrant thread of emotion. She needed him, he wanted her; he needed her, she wanted him; each needed and wanted the other with compelling intensity.

A groan of despair tore from Sean's throat as he ended the kiss. He continued holding her tightly against him. "The thought of you leaving is incomprehensible to me."

Erica lifted her head from his chest to look at his face. "We hardly know each other."

"We have to explore it," he said, his voice tinged with a peculiar sadness. "This thing between us. We have to see—"

"It makes no sense," she said. "You're an attorney. *My* attorney. What we're doing probably isn't even moral."

"There may be a question of ethics," he said, "but we're nowhere near approaching immorality."

"Ethics," Erica said. "That's what I meant. Should you . . . with a client?"

"Probably not," he said. "But, Erica, I don't feel this way about a woman often. Almost never. If either of us decides there's an ethical problem, your business can be easily transferred to someone else. But I'd hate to think that we might pass up something that could be truly meaningful to both of us because of a rule of professional ethics. When I kiss you, I'm not your lawyer. I'm—"

Erica drew away from him and turned her back to him. "That's the question, isn't it? What are you?" She turned to face him again. Her frustration poured out in the form of challenges that betrayed her confusion. "A kind stranger? A sympathy junkie? Does vulnerability turn you on? For all I know, you get the hots for any woman who's hurting or desperate."

"I meet a lot of hurting, desperate people in my work, many of them women. You're the first one I've ever held like this."

"Why me?" Erica said.

He combed his fingers into her hair and smiled. "Because your hair smells good." His thumb stroked her temple gently. "Because you have eyes a man could get lost in. Because. Just . . . because," he growled sensually.

Erica couldn't take her eyes from his. Her face burned under the intensity of his gaze.

He kissed her again, briefly but urgently, and she was breathless when he tore his mouth from hers and stepped back, putting an arm's length of space between them. Still looking at her face, he asked, "Any other dumb questions, Miss O'Leary?"

She shook her head.

"Good," he said with ingratiating sheepishness. "Now, which of those dozen things you have to do can I help with?"

"I've got to set the timers I bought, and get the cat in the carrier, and—" She tilted her head, listening as a car engine idled in the driveway. A few seconds later, the engine was cut off. "Damn!" she said, frowning. "That's Gary, and I'm not ready to go."

"Relax. What's he going to do, give you a detention for being tardy?"

"He's such a stickler about being on time."

"Marry him off," Sean said dryly. "A good woman will breed that out of him in no time."

"How many times have you been married?" she asked, realizing how little she knew about him.

His features and his voice hardened. "Just once."

If she'd had the time, she would have asked him, tenderly, what his ex-wife had done to make him so bitter, but Gary walked in the front door at that moment, and all opportunity for a private conversation was lost in the rustle of handshaking as the two men greeted each other.

"You must be here for the cat," Gary said. "I was sure glad to hear Erica had found someone to watch her. She was so frantic over what to do with Esmerelda that I was afraid I was going to have to sneeze and wheeze all the way back to Georgia." Rubbing his hands together, he turned to Erica. "Ready to hit the road?"

"Not quite," Erica said.

"She was asking my advice on the light timers," Sean said. "Why don't we set them while she gets the cat into the carrier."

"The lamps are already plugged into them," Erica said. "All you have to do is set the on and off hours."

Erica went to the master bedroom where she'd trapped Esmerelda earlier. The cat spent most of the time in the room, sleeping on the bed or pacing the floor, looking for her dead mistress. Catching the animal was no problem. All Erica had to do was sit down on the bed and the fat gray tabby was right beside her, nudging Erica's hands with her nose in a bid for attention. Erica let the cat climb into her lap. Esmerelda immediately rolled onto her back and meowed. "Poor kitty," Erica said, kneading the cat's chest. "You miss Gram as much as I do, don't you?"

Esmerelda responded with a loud purr.

"I hate having to send you off with a stranger, but you know how wheezy Gary gets when you go near him. Sean's a nice man. At least, I think he's a nice man. And he says he'll give you lots of attention, so—"

Resolutely, she scooped the cat into her arms and carried her to the travel case. "You'll be just fine," she said. "Just—" She caught sight of the cat's face through the small window just as the latch of the box clicked into place, and the creature's haunted eyes seemed to be asking for explanations. Erica choked back a sob. "Fine," she completed without conviction.

How could anything be fine when Gram was gone?

Determined not to cry—she'd done enough crying, especially in front of Sean O'Leary—she set her jaw and swallowed hard, then picked up the handle of the carrier. She followed the men's voices into the living room and paused to eavesdrop a moment, indulging her curiosity about what they were talking about. Seconds later, shaking her head, she walked through the hallway. She should have known! *The Orioles and the upcoming season. Baseball—what else?*

Stopping outside the living room, she saw Sean setting the last timer, while Gary stood nearby. "Here she is," she said. "Ready to go."

She knew the instant Sean's gaze locked with hers that he was aware of how close she was to tears. The man read her moods like the headlines of the morning newspaper. *And he said* she *could read minds!* "We'd better get her into your car before Gary starts—"

Gary produced a sneeze of timber-rattling proportions.

"Sneezing," Erica finished lamely.

"Go. Go!" Gary said tightly, waving toward the front door.

"He's really allergic," Sean mused aloud, sliding the carrier onto the back seat of his sedan.

"You can see why we couldn't take her to Georgia. Antihistamines would have been useless in a small car." She leaned over to tell the cat goodbye, then righted herself.

Sean put his hands on her shoulders. "I'll take good care of her."

"I know. It's just—"

"Your grandmother loved her."

Afraid she would burst into tears if she tried to speak, Erica nodded.

Sean cradled her face in his hands and studied it. "I have this recurring nightmare that I'll never meet you when you're not in an emotionally taxing situation."

"I don't know how I would have gotten through all this if you hadn't been so nice." She closed her eyes, sighed, then opened them again. "If you'd been a typical attorney, all formal and arrogant, or if you'd made a grab for me that night on the train instead of holding me the way you did."

"You'd have made it," he said. "You're stronger than you think you are."

"You were . . . compassionate."

"I'm glad I was able—" He growled in frustration. "Oh, hell, I'm not going to pussyfoot around this. I want to see you when you get back to Baltimore. I want to sit down with you where we can talk and get to know each other. You know what I'm trying to say."

Erica nodded.

Sean touched his lips to hers briefly. "We'll keep in touch."

6

SEAN WAS BEGINNING to regret his decision not to stop at the Dixie Fuel and Homestyle Chicken Deli to ask directions to the school where Erica taught when he spotted the marquee sign identifying Suwannee Elementary School and welcoming parents to field day. Impulsively, he turned into the crowded parking lot and eased his rented compact into one of the few empty spaces. He took the key from the ignition and stared at the tag identifying the make, model and license number of the rental car, somewhat astounded to find himself in the parking lot of an elementary school in Georgia instead of at his office in Towson.

What the hell had gotten into him? Rescheduling appointments, making flight arrangements less than twenty-four hours before a trip, throwing clothes into a suitcase and arranging for his housekeeper to look after things at home while he was gone—all to surprise a woman who might or might not be happy to have him show up to tell her happy birthday. He could plead temporary insanity and no one would argue with him.

Insanity, thy name is Erica, he thought. He hadn't gone a single waking hour without thinking of her since she'd left Maryland. Then, yesterday, when he was still holding on to a modicum of sanity, he'd glanced down at some papers he was going over and discovered on one of them that it was the eve of her birthday. He hadn't actually *decided* to drop everything on the spur of the moment and fly across four states to surprise her like a wet-behind-the-ears college student any more than he'd *decided* to stop at the jewelry store on the way home from his office to buy her a present. He'd simply sprung into action as though he were an automaton programmed to behave like a lovesick fool.

It's not too late, he told himself. *Just start up the car and drive right back to the airport, and she'll never know you were here. You'll be out the cost of the plane ticket and the car rental, but you'll still have your dignity.*

Dignity, schmignity! He was less than a football field's length away from Erica. He could hear the cheering of young voices, some of them undoubtedly those of her students, from the playground on the opposite side of the school. He really would be a lunatic if he turned back now. Every man had a right to make a fool of himself at least once, he told himself.

Shoving the keys into his pocket and setting his jaw, he stalked to the main entrance of the wide, flat building and walked in. A miasma of crayon, glue stick, tempera paint, powdered hand soap and lunchroom odors assailed his nostrils as he walked past glass-covered bulletin boards displaying student art and essays on his way to the administrative office.

A harried-looking woman behind the desk nodded as he approached. "You must be here for field day," she said with a distinct Georgia drawl. "Sign that sheet and write your name on one of those visitors' tags. Everybody's out on the sports field. You can put your children's names and grades on the tag if you like."

The hair on the back of Sean's neck bristled. "My children's names?"

"You *are* a parent, aren't you?"

Sean drew in a breath. "Actually, I don't have a child in this school. I was hoping to see Miss O'Leary. If it's parents only—"

"Our teachers are allowed to have guests, too. As long as you sign in." Her gaze, both curious and suspicious, settled on the clipboard he'd just signed. "Mr. O'Leary?" She lifted her head to eye him long and hard. "Are you Miss O'Leary's brother?"

Sean flashed her a charming smile. "We're not related. I'm her attorney. I was just passing through and thought I'd say hello."

"Not many folks 'just pass through' this town unless they take a wrong turn between Savannah and Augusta," she observed wryly.

"It *was* a bit of a detour," he admitted.

The secretary swallowed the questions she obviously wanted to ask. "Go out this door, turn left and walk straight through the building to get to the sports field. Miss O'Leary's in the third-grade area. Just look for shirts with pigs on them."

"Pigs?"

"The kids have been pig crazy ever since that movie, *Babe*. They choose their names for field day, and we have the Reynolds Pigs in fifth grade, the Hudson Hogs in second and the O'Leary Porkers in third."

Sean smiled and peeled the backing from the name tag and pressed the sticky side onto his shirt before heading toward the door.

"Enjoy your visit to Suwannee Elementary," the secretary drawled.

"That'll depend on how much Miss O'Leary likes surprises," he said, pausing in the doorway to answer the woman's brilliant smile with an affable grin.

The playground had been divided into clearly marked areas for each grade. Sean joined the throng of parents watching the third-graders, who were blissfully engaged in a contest involving balloons filled with slimy green goop. Lined up shoulder to shoulder in two parallel lines, they were tossing balloons filled with the goop back and forth, each line taking a step back after each toss so they were gradually farther and farther apart. When a balloon popped, the tosser lined up for another round of tosses, and the catcher, usually covered with green slime, joined green-smeared peers to cheer on their classmates as the event continued.

He spied Erica almost immediately, herding the children in line to toss the balloons in the next round. She was wearing jeans and an oversize T-shirt decorated with a cartoon pig on the front, and her hair was pulled up into two ponytails. Scarcely a foot taller than most of the pupils, she looked like one of them—except for her obviously adult curves. Rather than concealing her figure, the baggy shirt draped and clung in all the right places to emphasize the fullness of her breasts and the flare of her hips.

She had not escaped the scourge of the green slime. Her shirt and jeans were stained and there was a generous smear of goop on her left cheek. Standing at the waist-high rope that had been strung to keep the spectators off the field, Sean ached with the need to touch her. Hidden among the parents, he observed her for some time. Her attentiveness to her students was obvious in the way she bent over slightly when she listened to them and looked them squarely in the eye when she spoke to them.

When there were only a few pairs left on the field, tossing their balloons back and forth from the maximum distance until an unlucky catch resulted in a messy explosion of green, Erica walked down the line of students waiting for the next round, passing out new balloons from a plastic bucket. The children picked them up with varying degrees of bluster and bravado, one dipping his hand into the bucket for a reckless grab, another reaching in with the same nonchalance he'd use plucking a cookie from a cookie jar.

"That's my daughter," an attractive woman standing near Sean told the woman beside her. "That's Shonna."

The child she referred to, a beautiful little girl with expressive eyes and an infectious smile, was wearing an O'Leary Porkers shirt with the same cartoon pig on it as Erica's.

"My son's back toward the end of the line," the second mother said. "He's in Miss O'Leary's class, too. Don't you like her?"

"I surely do," the girl's mother replied. "She's been so good for Shonna—she's a little shy, and Miss O'Leary knows how to bring her out."

Shonna eased both hands into the bucket and brought out a jiggly balloon, cradling it in her small hands with the same caution she might a live grenade. Smiling, Erica said something to the girl that made her grin from ear to ear as she looked over at her mother and held up the balloon. In her zeal, she must have squeezed it with her fingers, because it burst, spewing green slime over her and Erica.

Horror-struck, the child looked up at her teacher, wide-eyed. Recovering from her surprise, Erica pulled her shirt away from her body and regarded the huge green blotch on the front and laughed. Relieved, Shonna giggled and turned to see if her mother had seen what happened.

Erica followed the child's gaze. Sean knew the instant she recognized him because her laughter faltered. He held his breath as he waited to see what her next reaction was then released it in a rush of relief when the laughter was replaced by a wide smile.

"Miss O'Leary!"

Erica had been so astounded to see Sean that she'd forgotten where she was and what she was doing. She blinked to attention and looked down at the student trying to get her attention. "Shonna? I'm sorry. What did you say?"

"Do I get another balloon or am I out because that one broke?"

"That one didn't count," Erica said, tilting the bucket within the child's reach. "Take another one." Half expecting to discover she'd been mistaken, she glanced at Sean again. *What was he doing here?*

She continued casting him intermittent questioning looks as she distributed the rest of the balloons and then, at the signal from Mary Jane White, the teacher directing the event, she marched the newly armed contestants onto the field for the next round of tossing. When they were lined up, she sent in their partners, one by one. "You're with Jason. You're with Tracy. You're with Angela—"

"Aw, Miss O'Leary. Do I have to be with a *girl?*" Tim Scott grumbled.

"You do if you want to be in this event," Erica said firmly. She had a similar conversation with another boy before everyone was paired off and ready for the starting whistle. She gave Mary Jane a nod, then walked over to the closest of two teachers supervising the students who'd been eliminated in the previous rounds. "Can you watch the line for me a few minutes?" she asked Karen Beck. "There's someone I need to talk to."

"No problem," Karen said. "I'm ready for a change of scenery."

She discovered Sean looking at her when she turned around. She'd known he would be. Smiling, she crossed the far end of the field and followed the rope, nodding greetings to parents along the way, until she came face-to-face with him. There, a foot in front of him, peering deeply into his eyes, she suddenly found herself speechless.

Obviously enjoying her predicament, Sean grinned. "Happy birthday, Miss O'Leary,"

She shook her head in disbelief. "H-how?"

"Airplane," he replied.

"But—why? What are you doing here?"

He leaned forward so no one else would hear. "You really don't want me to answer that in front of all these people, do you?"

Erica shook her head again. *If the glint in his eye was any indication of how he would answer her, she dared not ask for any demonstrations—especially when the glint in his eye affected her the way it did.*

His grin grew into a genuine smile. "I was sitting at my desk yesterday thinking about you and I glanced down at a paper that had your birth date on it. It clicked that tomorrow—which is now today—is your birthday, so I booked a morning flight and . . . here I am."

"But today, of all days! I must look like—"

"A pig?" he asked, noting the cartoon image on the front of her shirt, and then he smiled again. "You're the prettiest Porker I've ever seen." He leaned forward again. "I'm having a hard time keeping my hands off you."

The feeling was mutual. She was half an impulse away from flinging her arms around his neck and kissing him until he passed out from passion or exhaustion, whichever came first.

"Please tell me you don't have a hot date tonight."

"I do now," she said, meeting his intense gaze. *Real hot.* They stared at each other a moment. "I . . . uh, have to get back," she said, tilting her head toward the field.

"What's next?"

"The winners of this round get to slime the teachers."

"Again?" he teased, reaching up to wipe the smudge from her cheek with his thumb.

His magical touch reverberated through her entire body, hot and tingly. "Oh, Sean," she whispered.

"I know," he said with a bittersweet smile.

Another moment passed in charged silence. He pulled his hand away from her face and dropped his arm to his side. "Go on—get slimed. I'll be here cheering."

Still tingling from their encounter, she crossed the field again, aware of his eyes on her as she moved. She took several deep breaths as she walked, hoping to achieve an aura of calm before she reached Karen. *Were her cheeks as red as they were hot?*

Karen confirmed as much. "*Who* is that?" she asked the moment Erica was within earshot. It was no simple question. It was a demand for information.

"My grandmother's attorney," Erica said.

"Your grandmother's attorney?" Karen repeated dubiously. "From Baltimore?"

"He . . . uh, came to wish me a happy birthday."

"From Baltimore?"

"He . . . wants to take me out tonight," Erica said. "Do you think everyone's going to be okay with that? I mean, if I cancel out on dinner?"

"Well, I don't know," Karen said. "Gee, they might never forgive you for giving up dinner with people you see all day long, five days a week, to entertain a man who came all the way from Baltimore to tell you happy birthday. I'm sure they won't understand at all. Just because he's drop-dead gorgeous—"

"All right," Erica said. "You've made your point."

"What they're *not* going to forgive is that you've been keeping this hunk a secret."

"There's not . . . it's complicated," Erica said. "I wouldn't know where to begin. Will you explain to the others about dinner?" Involuntarily, her eyes went to Sean's face. "I'm not sure I'll get a chance—"

"Sure," Karen said. "But we'll expect a full report at the coffee station tomorrow morning. If you show up tomorrow."

"If I show up?"

"There are such things as personal-leave days, you know. If things work out, you shouldn't think twice about taking one. The kids are going to be wrung-out after today, anyway. Tim! Jason! If you two don't quit shoving, you're not going to get to participate in sliming the teachers." She turned to Erica again. "Whose idea was this teacher-slime thing anyway?"

"Mrs. Nutting's."

"I should have known. The slime queen herself."

"We don't have enough parents who want to get involved, to turn away an enthusiastic mother just because of a little thing like a cornstarch and lime-gelatin fetish," Erica said.

"Oh, well—the kids love it," Karen said philosophically. "Speaking of the teacher slime—"

Mary Jane was announcing the end of the balloon-toss event and asking the third-grade teachers to line up opposite those students who'd survived the final round.

"Tell me again why Mary Jane doesn't have to stand out here and get slimed," Karen said as they donned swim goggles.

"Because she's the third-grade team leader," Erica said, feeling like an absolute fool standing in the center of the field wearing goggles while her superior armed the students with detergent bottles filled with Mrs. Nutting's cornstarch-and-gelatin slime. What would Sean think?

She looked at him. He was watching her, grinning. She responded with a self-conscious grin.

He smiled broadly.

She laughed.

So did he.

If not for the two gallons of green slime flying in her direction from a dozen detergent bottles reminding her otherwise, she might have believed that she and Sean were the only two people on earth.

The kids were going crazy, cheering on the students who'd been lucky enough to win the opportunity to create havoc with their bottles of slime. The children's laughter was contagious, and the parents who weren't laughing were at least sporting smiles.

Sean's attention remained focused on Erica. There she was, lined up with her fellow teachers, the shortest and smallest of the bunch, the runt of the third-grade teaching team, her O'Leary Porker shirt covered with slime.

His heart swelled with admiration and respect. He felt a consuming need to protect her, a ravenous desire to touch her in every possible way, a poignant yearning to be alone with her.

He recognized the fullness of heart, the fascination, the need, the yearning. He'd felt it before, but only once. It was *love.*

Suddenly, everything made sense. He hadn't lost his mind, only his heart. His impulsive trip to surprise her was not the illogical act of a madman, it was a grand romantic gesture. A man in love was not expected to be logical, only devoted.

"O'Leary? I thought that was you when I saw Erica talking to you, but I had to see for myself." Erica's friend, Gary Wisdom, was standing on the other side of the rope with his hand extended in friendship.

"Mr. Wisdom," Sean said, accepting the other man's gesture of greeting. "It's good to see you again." *So what if he lied a little.* There was a proprietary aspect in the vice principal's attitude which, if not possessive in a romantic context, was, at the very least, protective in a male-toward-female way. His sudden appearance made Sean feel as though his space had been violated, and the only person with whom Sean was interested in sharing his space today was Erica O'Leary.

"You're a long way from Baltimore," Gary said affably. "What brings you so far off the beaten path?"

"It's *who*," Sean replied. "And I don't think I have to spell her name."

Gary's eyes followed Sean's to Erica. "No. I guess you don't." He chuckled. "Of course! It's her birthday. They're getting ready to surprise her with a cake, but I'll bet your arrival was a bigger surprise."

Sean was saved the awkwardness of a response by the confusion following the official end of the teacher-sliming event. The teacher who'd been directing it—and consequently had escaped getting slimed—announced that the room mothers would be serving cupcakes and punch. Parents were invited to step over the barricade to join their children in their designated homeroom areas.

Tubs of water had been set up for washing hands, but aside from getting the children's hands clean enough to handle food, they made no real progress in turning grubby, slimy, sweaty little athletes into sweet, presentable children. Grubby, slimy teachers did not fare much better. When Sean reached Erica, he found her scrubbing her arms up to her elbows, but her face was almost as green as her eyes, and her hair was matted with gloopy green globs of slime.

Frowning, she said, "I can't believe you chose today to show up!"

"I got to see you in action," he replied.

She flicked the water from her hands and stood up. "Contrary to what you just observed, I don't usually spend my workdays being squirted with slime."

"Attention, third-graders," the teacher who'd been leading the balloon toss announced, using a bullhorn. "One of our teachers has a birthday today. Miss O'Leary, your students and your room mothers have a surprise for you."

Erica expressed gracious surprise when she was presented with a cake decorated with flaming candles while the entire third grade sang "Happy Birthday" to her. Sean stepped aside, downing a cupcake and a glass of punch while Erica greeted parents and talked to her students until the dismissal bell signaled the end of the school day. Then he pitched in with the clean-up efforts until Erica was ready to leave.

Her apartment was only half a mile from the school. He followed her there in the rental car and parked next to her. "Here it is," she said as she unlocked the door. "Home sweet home." She grinned. "I've been trying to remember if there are any dirty dishes sitting around."

"As if I'd give a damn," he said, emitting a sigh of relief as he stepped into the living room and heard the door click shut. "I was beginning to think I'd never get you alone."

"I'll get you all slimy!" she protested halfheartedly as he took her into his arms.

He only pulled her closer. "I traveled almost six hundred miles just to kiss you on your birthday. Do you think I'd let a little green stuff stop me?"

"Noooooo!" she cried jubilantly, throwing her arms around his neck and hugging him tightly.

There was no question of holding back. His frustrated need for her exploded in a hungry kiss that involved them totally. The punch had left an unexpected trace of fruity sweetness on her lips that tantalized his senses as his mouth covered hers. Her hands roved greedily and restlessly over his back and he traced her curves just as greedily and with equal restlessness. Her body was familiar to him; he'd memorized every slope and swell of it that night on the train.

The moment came when the kiss had to end or evolve into something much more consuming. Sean lifted his mouth from hers and they regarded each other with shy, self-conscious smiles. "Now you know why I flew half the length of the Eastern Seaboard to see you," he said.

Erica poised her mouth to speak then closed it, as though she wasn't sure what to say. Sean plucked a clump of green goo from her hair and grinned. "So where am I taking you tonight?"

"What did you have in mind?"

"You might want to rephrase that," he said drolly.

Erica swallowed. "What kind of place are you looking for?"

"Quiet, with good food and candlelight."

"There's only one place, then—Grogan's Folly."

"Odd name for a restaurant."

"It's an old mansion. That's what everyone's always called it, so the owners kept the name when they converted it. You can phone for reservations while I get cleaned up. The telephone directory is next to the phone in the kitchen. Oh, and look at your shirt." She brushed the front of it futilely. "I told you I'd get you all slimy."

"I've got a change of clothes in my suitcase. After I call the restaurant, I'll find a hotel and—"

"Don't be ridiculous! You don't have to go to a hotel. You're welcome to stay here if you don't mind humble accommodations. The couch makes into a perfectly good bed."

"Are you sure? I know it's a small town and your friends . . . if my spending the night here makes it awkward for you—"

"I'll get the third degree tomorrow no matter where you spend the night," she said.

"What will they want to know?"

"Everything."

"And what will you tell them?"

"As little as possible," she said, grinning. Then, looking down at her stained shirt, she shook her head. "I've *got* to take a shower and get out of these clothes before the health department hauls me off to the dump. Just . . . make yourself at home and help yourself to anything in the pantry or fridge."

Sean nodded. But what he wanted wasn't in the pantry or the fridge. What he wanted was going to be a few yards away behind a door under hot running water. He struggled to shake the image from his mind when he heard the water running.

He remembered enough about female rituals to know that bathing—or showering, as the case may be—meant more to a woman than simply cleansing the skin, and that getting dressed involved more than putting on clothes. But he'd forgotten what it was like to wait on a woman to complete those mysterious female rituals while anticipation gnawed at his guts.

Trying to tune out the sound of that running water and the inevitable images of droplets streaming over naked flesh and painting soap mosaics on slippery, steam-pinked skin, he located the directory and reserved a table for two at Grogan's Folly. Then he made another local call before phoning his office to check for messages. Relieved to find there were no crises to deal with there, he made one more call.

"It's me," he said to the woman who answered the phone. "I made it. I just wanted—"

"You worry too much," the woman said. "Everything and everyone here is fine. How about you? How'd your meeting go? Did you get everything worked out with the client you went to see?"

"I think I'm making some real progress," he replied.

"Good. Then it was worth the trip."

"Yes. I'm glad I came." He paused briefly. "I'll, uh, see you tomorrow as soon as my flight gets in."

The sound of running water had been replaced by the high-pitched whir of a hair dryer as he walked back into the living room. He went out to the rental car and brought in his bag, then stretched out on the sofa, sinking into the plump cushions as all the rushing around he'd had to do to make the early-morning flight caught up with him. His eyes drifted closed for a moment, until he was startled to alertness by something tickling his nose. He opened his eyes to discover an orange cat sniffing him curiously.

"Well, hello," he said, petting the cat's head. The animal meowed, tilted her head to accommodate his affection and stretched out on the narrow ledge of cushion between his chest and the edge of the sofa.

Just like Esmerelda, Sean thought wryly, careful not to push the feline off. *Of course, he'd much preferred cuddling with the cat's owner.*

Erica found him a while later and shook her head in dismay. Wasn't it just the story of her life? Here she was, scrubbed, combed and perfumed, and there was her romantic prince—sound asleep on her couch. With her cat!

She might have known Aunt Pitty-Pat would make a beeline to a warm, hard chest. *The little hussy!*

She seized the opportunity to study Sean's handsome face at leisure. He was totally relaxed. The laugh-and-squint lines around his eyes were less pronounced and his eyelashes, thick enough to make a princess green with envy, cast jagged shadows on his cheeks. His normally strong jaw was slack enough to part his lips slightly, and he made a ragged sound that was not quite a snore as he exhaled.

Despite the illusion of vulnerability and innocence sleep created, he remained large, strong and uncompromisingly male. Memories of the comfort she'd found in his arms, always when she'd most needed it, rushed through Erica's mind as she looked at him. She recalled his unquestioning compassion on the train, the strength he shared at the memorial service, his understanding at the park. No longer overwhelmed by fear or grief or shock, she now found herself drawn to the whole man.

A smile played at her mouth. *He was a man a woman could easily fall in love with.*

Maybe—just maybe—she was already a little in love with him.

An hour later, she knelt next to the couch and touched his hand. "Sean?"

He jerked awake. "Wha . . . ?"

"You fell asleep."

Pushing up on his right elbow and shoving his left hand through his hair, he said, "I'm sorry. I was trying not to disturb the cat. I guess I—"

"Don't apologize. You were really zonked. You must have been exhausted. I hated to disturb you, but—"

Reaching for her hand, he guided her onto his lap. His eyes caressed her face. "This is the second time I've woken up with you. I could get used to it."

Overwhelmed by the intimacy in his words, Erica buried her face on his shoulder. "The bathroom's all yours. I put out fresh towels."

"What time is it?" he asked.

"After five."

"I *did* sleep," he said with a soft groan. He turned his head and kissed her temple. "When I'm back in Baltimore, I'll regret wasting precious minutes I could have spent with you."

Sighing his name, she tilted her head back, inviting his kiss. It was an invitation he couldn't resist.

7

SEAN WAS ENGROSSED in the evening news on television when Erica strolled into the living room.

"I hope you don't mind if I watch—" His mouth dropped open as he looked in her direction.

"Watch what?" she asked with an enigmatic smile.

"You," he said, groping for the power switch on the remote control.

She crossed the room with deliberate slowness, conscious of his scrutiny as she moved. He stood up to greet her, holding his hands out to her. "That is *some* dress."

"This old thing?" she said, referring to the little black dress she saved for special occasions. She always felt feminine and sexy when she wore it. The off-the-shoulder neckline showed off her fair skin and narrow shoulders in a flattering way, and the flared, midthigh skirt showed her legs to advantage.

"There's just one thing missing," Sean said. He rummaged in the inside pocket of his coat and brought out a long, slender box. "This."

Erica hadn't been expecting a present, especially a small package with the name of a jewelry store emblazoned in a tasteful gold-foil label on the corner of the black-gloss wrapping paper. She ripped away the paper and opened the box with trembling fingers. A delicate gold bracelet with a single charm lay nestled in the deep purple velvet lining. Treating the bracelet with awe, she draped it across her hand, centering the miniature locomotive in her palm so she could examine it.

"It's stunning," she said, looking at Sean's face. "The detail—"

"Let's see if it fits." He picked up the bracelet and wrapped it around her wrist. His fingers grazed her skin as he fastened the clasp. Instead of letting go of her wrist, he guided it to his mouth, and their gazes locked as he kissed the sensitive area at the base of her palm. "It fits."

"It's perfect," she said. "I'll think of you every time I look at it."

He smiled sweetly. "I hope you look at it often, then."

Their eyes met for a long, heart-stopping moment. "You took a chance coming here, surprising me," she said.

"The trip was an impulse. I tried to talk myself out of it all the way to the airport, telling myself it was crazy. I knew it was a gamble, but I wanted to see you. I *needed* to see you."

"*Most* unlawyer-like," she observed.

"Most," he agreed.

"But you came, anyway."

He didn't flinch. "Yes."

"I'm glad," she said, accepting the fact that they were talking about a lot more than a single, impulsive decision.

"So am I."

They shared a moment of quiet understanding. Erica felt as though every nerve ending in her body had been mysteriously energized, making them supersensitive. She was so attuned to him, so aware of him and the attraction drawing them together that she was afraid to speak. Afraid to move. Afraid, almost, to breathe.

He said, "If I touch you now—"

Erica released the breath she was holding and moved her head in an almost imperceptible nod. *If he touched her, they would never make it to Grogan's Folly.*

THEY REACHED the restaurant just before sunset. Like an enchanted cottage, the old mansion reposed amid magnolia trees in full bloom. The fragrant white flowers shone in the lush, hunter green leaves like stars in a midnight sky. Climbing roses, wisteria, honeysuckle and jasmine bejeweled the mansion's trellises, and fuchsia hydrangea blossoms as big as bowling balls flanked the steps leading onto the restaurant's gingerbread veranda. The lemony scent of the magnolia, the grapelike scent of the wisteria and the sweet floral aromas of the roses and honeysuckle perfumed the air as they followed the stone-paved walkway to the veranda.

The closeness they had experienced on the train was between them again, but now there was something else in the equation. On the train, they had been two human beings, one in need of compassion, the other giving it. Now they were two human beings, one male, one female, each aware of the desire thrumming between them.

There was no menu to peruse, no choices to make regarding cuisine. Food appeared course by course, served by tuxedoed waiters who inquired after their comfort and offered assistance without chitchat that would have intruded on their privacy. Between courses, Sean reached across the table to cover her hand with his. "Are those peacocks?"

Erica followed his gaze to the lawn where two of the birds had wandered into range of a light mounted in a tree. She nodded.

"This place is incredible," he said. "Like something out of—"

"A fairy tale?" Erica asked. She'd felt as though she'd dropped into the pages of an illustrated fairy tale ever since Sean had shown up. Now they were living the finale. She was a twice rescued damsel in a sexy black dress, and Sean was the dashing prince in an elegant dark suit. He'd slain the dragons of desperation and sorrow for her; now he courted her in princely fashion.

Everything fed into the fantasy: their cozy table for two next to a window overlooking the sloping lawns; the candle bathing their faces in a mellow, romantic glow as the sun sank into the horizon beyond the magnolia trees; the whisper of classical music from a concealed sound system.

"Yes," he said. They were still watching the peacocks. The cock was trying to get the hen's attention and the hen was playing coy. Emitting an impatient shriek, the cock fanned his tail feathers into an arc of brilliant color and vibrated it as he strutted and danced.

Grinning, Sean turned back to Erica. "Do you suppose they get paid to put on that show?"

"I hope not," Erica said. "I'd rather believe that they're just—"

"Falling madly in love?" Sean teased.

"This would be the place for it," Erica said. "Grogan, the Yankee millionaire who built this place, had five daughters, so he deliberately set out to make Grogan's Folly a romantic place in order to marry them off. Apparently, the daughters needed all the help they could get in that area."

"Are you making this up?"

Erica chuckled. "No. That's why this place has always been called Grogan's Folly. The Grogan misses were reputed to be so homely that even the enticement of a generous dowry wasn't enough to draw suitors, so anytime a prospective groom appeared, Grogan made sure the atmosphere was conducive to romance. The whole story is in the brochure next to the door. You can pick one up on your way out."

"I won't need a brochure to remember tonight," he said. *And you, Miss O'Leary, require no atmosphere to make a man desire you.*

Erica feared his eyes would devour her as he looked at her across the table. Hoping to start a conversation before they ended up *on* the table, she said, "You haven't mentioned Esmerelda. How is she doing?"

"Esmerelda is spoiled rotten. She drives the housekeeper crazy chasing the broom and dust mop. I don't know where she sleeps at night, but the instant the alarm goes off, she's on the bed, sitting on my chest."

Erica laughed softly. "That sounds like Esmerelda." She took a sip of wine. "Cats seem to find you charming. Aunt Pitty-Pat doesn't curl up next to just anyone."

"Is that your cat's name—Aunt Pitty-Pat?"

"Like Scarlett's aunt. I got her in Atlanta when I was still in high school. She's getting old and crotchety now. I hope she and Esmerelda get along when I go back to Baltimore. Aunt Pitty-Pat isn't as spry as she used to be, and she's going to have trouble adjusting to a different house. If Esmerelda becomes territorial, it could be a long summer."

"When you say summer, do you mean the entire summer?" Sean asked hopefully.

"Most of it, at least," she said. "It'll take me that long to go through the house and decide what I want to keep and what needs to be sold or donated to charity." She sighed. "I'm not looking forward to it."

"Too many memories?"

She nodded. "I can't imagine what it's going to be like."

His thumb rubbed over the tops of her fingers. "If you ever need—"

"You can't keep rescuing me, Sean. I have to work through my grandmother's death on my own."

The waiter arrived with plates of roast turkey, corn bread dressing and candied sweet potatoes. Sean partook of the robust Southern fare appreciatively, confessing that he'd had nothing to eat all day except a croissant on the airplane and the cupcake at the school.

Between the entrée and the dessert, Erica slipped off her shoe and rubbed her toes back and forth against the inside of Sean's ankle and watched the surprise register on his face. Desire burned in his eyes as their gazes locked, and an answering heat curled through her, starting in her womb and radiating upward and outward.

She declined dessert, but let Sean feed her a forkful of the rich pecan pie from his plate. The gesture of sharing his food with her, primitive and instinctual, was more intimate than a kiss. She felt full and flushed, swollen with desire. Her awareness of him grew with each look, each touch.

As they walked to the car, he stretched his arm across her back and his long fingers molded the curve of her ribs. Stopping next to the car, he turned to face her and peered into her eyes. "I didn't come here to seduce you," he said.

But his hand came up to cradle her face as tenderly as he would a flower. "Do you think about that night, too, Erica?" he asked. "When you're on the verge of sleep, do you remember what it was like when we were together, close to each other, touching each other?"

"Every night," she admitted in a hoarse whisper.

He pushed her hair away from her face. "Then I'm not crazy."

He covered her mouth in a kiss that fanned the desire shifting through her into greedy fingers of fire. An eternity passed before he lifted his head and wordlessly opened the car door for her.

Neither said a word on the twenty-minute drive back to her apartment. After parking the car, Sean cut the engine and exhaled heavily before getting out and walking around the car to open her door. He put his arm across her back again and walked her to her door.

"What?" Erica said as they turned the corner and her apartment came into view. There, in front of her door, was a large stuffed pig holding a bouquet of foil Happy Birthday balloons with ribbon streamers.

"Happy birthday, Miss O'Leary," Sean said as she turned to him.

She leaped into his arms, throwing her own around his neck, her lips finding his mouth with unerring instinct. They kissed like lovers who'd been involuntarily parted for years, like clandestine lovers stealing passion in an alley, like people who'd just narrowly escaped death together.

They were both heaving for breath when Sean pulled back. "We'd better decide on the sleeping arrangements before you open that door," he said.

"We were strangers on the train," she said. "We're not strangers anymore."

Sean slid his hands to her upper arms and looked down at her face. "Erica—"

His hesitation contradicted the desire in his eyes. Confused by his reticence, Erica said, "I thought—" The statement ended on a sigh. "Are you having second thoughts about coming here?"

He took several labored breaths before answering, "Would you believe I'm nervous?"

"I could believe I am," she said. "But you?" *Not after the way they'd kissed.* She shook her head. "If there's a reason you're holding back—a wife you've neglected to divorce or a fiancée you've conveniently forgotten, tell me now."

He drew her into a tight hug. "I don't have a wife, Erica. Or a fiancée. And I don't have any intention of holding back." Hot, hard and strong, his body confirmed the words. His desire for her was undeniable. His heat burned into her, his hardness aroused her, his strength surrounded her. "I haven't felt this way about a woman in a long time," he continued. "The whole thing has been a bit overwhelming for me. I showed up today unannounced. I don't want to overwhelm you or rush you into anything."

"Too late," she said, tilting her head back so she could make eye contact with him. "I'm already overwhelmed."

The door opened with a click. She picked up the stuffed pig and balloons in one hand and weaved the fingers of her other hand through his then led him to the bedroom. There, she freed the balloons from the weight of the pig, letting them float to the ceiling, trailing the rainbow of ribbons.

"The fairy tale continues," she said, placing the pig on the bedside table before opening the small drawer on the front of the table and bringing out a foil-wrapped condom, which she pressed into Sean's palm. Grinning, she said, "Here. You can take care of the reality."

He stared at the small package a moment as though he'd never seen one before then nodded tersely and placed it on the table, where it would be within easy reach.

An awkward silence followed.

"You really *are* nervous, aren't you?" Erica said, raising her arms and draping her wrists on his shoulders.

Sean frowned self-consciously.

"Does it help to tell you that I am, too?" she asked.

His gaze met hers. "With me?"

She kissed him then, softly, tenderly, testing the shape and texture of his lips as though they'd never kissed before. Gradually, he took control. His lips became bolder, demanding and urgent. His mouth left hers to explore her jawline. Erica tilted her head back, inhaled sharply and tightened her arms around him as he teased her neck with nibbling kisses.

The trail of kisses continued along her shoulder until he reached the top of her dress. He moved his lips to her other shoulder, and then along the neckline of the dress, across the tops of her breasts.

Erica worked down the knot of his tie, passed it over his head and frivolously looped it around a decorative vase on the night table. Then she pulled his shirt free of his pants, unbuttoned it and slid it over his shoulders. It hung up where the cuffs fit his wrists snugly. "You're at my mercy now," she said.

"I've been at your mercy since the first time I smelled your hair," he said. "But go ahead and—"

"Torture you?" She leaned over and kissed his bare midriff.

Sean grumbled a shocking expletive.

"Begging for mercy already?" she taunted, then flicked her tongue across his skin before unfastening the cuff links binding his sleeves at his wrists. She freed his shirt and tossed it aside, then walked to the bed, folding back the comforter and top sheet in appealing invitation. Presenting her back to Sean, she instructed him to unzip her dress and slipped the garment off before climbing into bed between the sheets. Stretching out on her side, she pushed up on one elbow, and smiled shyly. "Kick off your shoes, O'Leary, and stay a while."

She admired his solid male body as he took off his shoes and slid his pants down and off his long, beautifully muscled legs. "What? No shamrocks and leprechauns?" she asked.

His gaze followed hers to the front of his briefs, stretched taut over his aroused flesh. Embarrassed, he swallowed, then cleared his throat like a Victorian schoolmaster. "This time when I packed, the laundry was done."

He got into bed, stretching out beside her and rolling so he could see her face. The hint of a grin, self-conscious and smug, played at his mouth, and Erica responded with a tentative smile. For an immeasurable interval, time hung suspended while Erica wondered what to do, whether to touch him, *where* to touch him, *how* to touch him, knowing they were on the verge of an inferno.

Without warning, Sean grabbed the edge of the bedding and yanked it up over his head. Erica pursed her lips to ask what he was doing, but before she could utter "What," she was being pulled under with him. Sensation took over in the sudden darkness as he rolled her under him and his mouth sought hers, placing impatient kisses across her forehead and over her cheek before molding her lips.

His chest crushed her breasts, his thighs rubbed hers and his hands caressed and kneaded with restless impatience, tracing the subtle taper of her back down to her waist and up to her shoulders again while his tongue plundered her mouth.

Glorying in his touch, Erica explored and savored the textures of him, as well, the smoothness of skin, the coarseness of male hair, the curve of firm muscles.

The combined heat from their bodies created a sweltering atmosphere under the bedding. Sean flung back the covers cocooning them and lifted his head and they both gulped for air. Erica cradled his cheeks in her palms and, smiling sweetly, murmured his name. Mesmerized, he stared mutely at her flushed cheeks, her lips still swollen from their kiss, her wildly mussed hair.

"I had forgotten," he said. *Forgotten how beautiful an aroused woman could be. Forgotten how a man could think he couldn't want a woman any more than he wanted her, and then discover that he wanted her ten times that much when he realized he was going to have her. Forgotten what it was like to burn with a need so fierce that only regard for the woman he was with held the wild animal within in check.*

"Let's see if I can refresh your memory," she invited, teasing his ears with her thumb.

His gaze slid down to her chest and he traced the edge of her lace bandeau with his forefinger. She released a shuddering sigh as he drew an imaginary line on her flushed skin, then cooed sensually when he pushed the top edge of the stretch bra down and retraced the line a quarter of an inch lower.

He was going to look at her breasts, feel them. Erica trembled with anticipation. *Touch them . . . kiss them—*

The seconds he took in doing it seemed more like hours. She heard his sharp inhalation as he saw her for the first time, felt her nipples pebble as his hot breath slid over them. Then he covered her right breast, and she arched, pressing the lush fullness into his palm.

Kneading her flesh, he whispered her name. She moaned in pleasure, and undulated restlessly beneath him.

Sean responded with a growl of sheer male arousal and worked her panty hose down over her hips, her thighs. Erica kicked them the rest of the way off, her every movement enticing as her bare thigh rubbed his. Sean kissed his way to her other breast and drew on it, then flicked the sensitive tip with his tongue.

Wedging his leg between hers, he slid his hand from her knee, up the side of her thigh and back down, massaging with his thumb. His hot, hard flesh pressed against her hip, persistently telegraphing his readiness for her.

"Kiss me," she pleaded breathlessly, guiding his head back to her face.

The kiss was amazingly gentle, yet it seemed to go on forever as Sean breached her panties and his fingers delved into secret, private places.

They grew frenzied, exploring each other desperately until, finally, he joined their bodies in a savagely gentle thrust. Together, they sought release in instinctive movements, rhythmic, frantic and mindlessly urgent. Together, they made the frenetic, terrifying, tumultuous journey to physical ful-fillment.

Clinging to him, arching against him, Erica cried out as the fiery talons of desire finally released her from their grip. Sean followed quickly, his arms convulsing around her as a feral growl tore from his throat before the tension in his body gave way to euphoric lethargy.

Time held no relevance for either of them. Caught in an embrace of body, mind and soul, they held each other while their hearts slowed to normal and air found its way in and out of their lungs without strain. At last he eased his weight off her and lay next to her, holding her in his arms. Erica rested her cheek on his chest. Her breasts, still tingling, com-pressed against his ribs. Her leg, bent at the knee, stretched across his thighs. She released a lazy sigh that bespoke pro-found contentment.

"I've never even heard a cat sigh like that," Sean com-mented.

"Have you ever made love to a cat?" she murmured, the words dancing warmly through the hair on his chest.

"No," he said with a chuckle.

"That's why," she said. She yawned and snuggled closer. "Why'd you have to be a lawyer?"

Sean rubbed his cheek back and forth against her hair without replying. Minutes later, she fell asleep, but except for a few nodding-off intervals, Sean didn't sleep. He could sleep all those lonely nights when the bed seemed as large as a con-tinent and empty as a witch's heart, and he ached for a woman, body and soul—all those lonely nights that he didn't have Erica next to him.

She stirred when his travel alarm beeped at four-thirty and mumbled, "Make . . . breakfast—"

Sean kissed her cheek. "Go back to sleep. They'll feed me on the plane—not that I need a plane to soar to Baltimore after last night."

He'd thought she was asleep, but he must have been only half-right, because she cuddled closer and sighed. "You shouldn't say such sweet things. Now I have to think about you while we're apart."

"You'd better," he said, kissing her earlobe. He held her another few minutes before easing out of bed. After dressing, he stole back to the side of the bed to look at her one more time before leaving. The vision took his breath away. Her face was relaxed in sleep. Her hand lay on the pillow, small and delicate with her graceful fingers and rosy polished nails. The bracelet he'd given her circled her wrist and the charm reposed on the pillowcase, a golden silhouette on the smooth fabric.

He didn't risk waking her with a kiss, but he left knowing he was leaving part of his heart behind.

8

THE NEXT FEW WEEKS were the most hectic of Erica's life. In addition to being in the throes of the manic, end-of-school-year marathon of paperwork and emotional farewells from her students, she had to prepare for her extended stay in Baltimore. It was the first time since graduating from college and having her own apartment that she would be spending an entire summer away, and she discovered that there were a million and one things to do.

Despite all her rushing around, Sean had been in her thoughts constantly. In the classroom, the teachers' lounge, her car, her apartment, in lines at the supermarket and the bank, she'd rubbed the tiny gold train on the bracelet he had given her, recalling with sweet detail the time they'd spent together.

She had talked to him nightly since his trip to Georgia. Their conversations were not the least mushy or sentimental, yet there was an underlying communication between their words, unspoken messages in their routine phrases and the questions that pepper such phone calls. "How are you?" meant, *Do you miss me?* "How was your day?" asked, *Did you think of me?* "It was hectic" implied the silent endearment, *But I thought of you anyway.*

"I miss you" was the most loaded euphemism of all, packed with degrees of meaning on a myriad of levels: *I miss your smile. Your voice. Your face. The way you look at me. The way you touch me.*

They were lovers. When she thought about it rationally, with so many miles separating them, it seemed incredible that she had become so deeply involved with a man she'd known such a short time, especially an attorney. Yet, as incredible as it was, it seemed equally as inevitable. A bond had formed between them that night on the train. Before they were lovers, before she'd told him her name, before he'd known she was the granddaughter of his client, they had come together as two people; she, with an overwhelming need for compassion; he, with the sensitivity to recognize that need and the generosity to fill it.

SHE MADE IT to Towson just ahead of the afternoon rush-hour traffic on the second day of driving. Sean had told her he'd have someone get her grandmother's house ready for her arrival, and he'd kept his word. She opened the door to the scents of lemon furniture polish and fresh flowers. The blinds had been opened to admit sunlight, the refrigerator plugged in and stocked with bottled water. And a massive bouquet of spring flowers sat in the center of the dining-room table.

Erica had expected that Ardeth Maxwell might leave cut flowers from the greenhouse somewhere in the house, but instinct told her that she'd find a florist's card tucked in *this* arrangement. Her instincts proved correct. She read the card, pressed it over her heart and sighed. It said: Tomorrow night. Eight o'clock. Sean.

The phone rang as she was carrying in the last of several boxes she'd labeled as miscellaneous. Leaving the box in the entryway, she dashed to answer it.

"You made it," Sean said in response to her hello.

"Safe and sound," she said, adding wearily, "and tired."

"I thought you would be," he said. "I had hoped to rescue you and feed you tonight, but I have something I can't reschedule."

"It's just as well," she said. "I'm a zombie." As anxious as she was to see him, she was glad she didn't have to face him after two days of driving. She would get settled in the house, sleep late in the morning, finish unpacking and still have time to pamper herself and primp before their date. After the past few weeks, she deserved a little pampering.

"If I didn't have this thing tonight," he told her, "I'd come over and give you a back rub."

"Don't tease me," she said. "Mentioning a back rub to a woman who's been in a car for two days is as cruel as waving a chocolate éclair under the nose of someone on a diet."

"You're in an interesting mood. Almost whimsical."

"Exhaustion has made me light-headed," she said, but she knew it wasn't exhaustion from her trip influencing her mood, but exhilaration from hearing his voice. Knowing he was in the same city and she would see him in just over twenty-four hours had buoyed her sagging spirits.

They talked a while longer, firming up their plans to go to dinner the next evening. Erica hung up the phone with a smile on her face. *They were going to start with dinner, but she'd be willing to bet her new red lace teddy that dessert would be spectacular!*

After unpacking her suitcases, she took a long bath, and put on an old T-shirt and a pair of shorts. Then she called out for pizza, which she ate while watching a tabloid news show on television. Afterward, she stretched out on the couch to watch a movie she'd seen half a dozen times. Aunt Pitty-Pat, who'd been poking her whiskers into every nook and cranny of the strange house, abandoned her exploration to curl next to Erica for a nap, purring contentedly while Erica absently stroked the feline's neck.

The phone rang, startling them both. Aunt Pitty-Pat leaped up, shook herself and stared accusingly at Erica.

"I didn't do it!" Erica protested as she reached for the phone on the end table. "It's probably either a wrong number or a weirdo. Hello?"

"Erica? It's Sean. I managed to get away a little earlier than I expected, and I decided to see if your lights were still on."

"My lights?" Erica said. "Where *are* you?"

"About a block away from your house. Are you up to that back rub?"

"I—" She laughed nervously. "Yes, but—"

"I'm circling the block then. I'll be at your door in about two minutes."

"Two minutes?" She looked down at her faded shirt.

"Three minutes, tops," he said. "See you then."

She heard the click as the connection was severed and frowned at the receiver before replacing it, then turned her exasperation to Aunt Pitty-Pat. "The man is a maniac! Two minutes!" Her eyes widened. "Two minutes! Damn!"

Heedless of the cat, she scurried off the sofa and dashed to the bathroom, grimacing when she saw herself in the mirror. She wasn't sure what to reach for first, but she quickly brushed her teeth and applied some lipstick, then attacked her hair with styling gel and intense determination. It wasn't perfect, but it was passable by the time Sean knocked.

He was standing on her doorstep, his elbow propped against the jamb and one leg casually crossed in front of the other, grinning like a mischievous child and eyeing her like a hungry rabbit sizing up a carrot. *He*, of course, was gorgeously disheveled. He'd left his coat in the car. His top shirt button was open, the knot of his tie loosened as though he simply refused to wear it a second longer than absolutely necessary—a potent cross between a little boy who'd tolerated a suit as long as he could stand it and a full-grown, virile male who'd left business at the office and now had more important things on his mind.

"I see you weren't always a Porker," he commented, looking at the front of her shirt.

Erica stepped aside to let him in. "The first year I taught, my class was the O'Leary Rexes."

"As in, Tyrannosaurus rex?"

She nodded.

"Nice shirt," he said wryly.

"I wasn't expecting company."

"Actually," he said, "I like it."

She grasped the tail of the shirt on either side and pulled it out, stretching it several inches in both directions. "You're just blinded by glamour."

"I'm blinded by your lack of need for it." He pulled her into his arms. "We'll be glamorous tomorrow night. Tonight—"

He kissed her briefly. Erica slid her arms around his waist and rested her cheek on his chest. Sean's hands roved over her back soothingly. "Tonight I'm playing masseur, remember."

"Promises, promises," she murmured, rolling her shoulder and uttering a contented little sound as he located a particularly tight muscle and rubbed it in circular strokes. "Mmm," she purred. "You've done this before."

"My wife worked as a secretary when I was in law school. I used to get the kinks out of her shoulders."

Erica jerked away abruptly.

"I'm sorry," he said, obviously contrite. "That was stupid of me."

"It sounded so . . . immediate."

"It was a long time ago," he said. "Erica, I haven't had a wife or given a back rub in over three years."

She allowed him a small smile. "But who's counting, right?"

Sean tried to hide how badly the words hurt. *Who's counting?* How often had he asked himself the same question, always knowing the answer? *He* was counting, and he had been for a long, long time. *Too long.*

Long enough. His being here with Erica, thinking only of her, was proof of that.

Thank God. Maybe now he could stop counting.

He wanted to explain what his being with her meant, but in this moment of realization he just wanted to hold her and bask in the freedom. "You really should lie down for this," he said.

"On the floor?"

"The couch will do. On your stomach, please. Use one of those pillows to get your head in a comfortable position. That is, if you can get that beast to give up possession."

Aunt Pitty-Pat had taken a position of occupation on the sofa and glared at them as though daring them to try to move her. Erica scooped the cat into her arms and rubbed the feline's chest. "She's still a little hyper from the trip."

"I didn't come straight from the house, or I would have brought Esmerelda," Sean said.

"If you wouldn't mind keeping her a few more days, I'd kind of like to let Aunt Pitty-Pat get used to the house before I bring in a second cat."

"Esmerelda can stay as long as she likes," Sean replied, scratching Aunt Pitty-Pat behind the ears. "We've gotten used to having her around."

Erica put the cat down and stretched out on the sofa, plumping a throw pillow beneath her cheek as she made herself comfortable. Sean sat beside her, wedging his hip in the inward curve of her waist. "Just relax," he said. "Take some deep breaths."

The subtle chafing of her ribs against his buttocks as she inhaled was sweet torture. He tucked her hair to one side and began kneading her neck with his fingertips.

"There's a bottle of body lotion on the end table," she said.

Sean squeezed a dab of the lotion onto her nape, and she gasped. "That's cold! You're supposed to warm it in your hands first."

"What's wrong, O'Leary—can't take it?"

"You could have warned me," she grumbled, but there was no rancor in the complaint.

He spread the lotion and then massaged it into her skin with circular strokes. After a moment, she exhaled a lengthy sigh, and said languidly, "Your wife was crazy to divorce you."

Sean froze, wondering how to tell her there had been no divorce. "This stuff smells like peaches," he said.

"It's called Peaches and Cream," she replied absently.

He slid his fingers inside the ribbing on the neck of her shirt and moved his thumbs down her spine from her nape, then outward along her shoulder as far as the fabric allowed. After a few minutes, satisfied that the tension in her shoulders was reduced, he withdrew his hands.

She moaned in protest. "You can't stop now," she said huskily. "You've only rubbed away the first two hundred miles."

"You're a demanding woman, Erica O'Leary," he said, but her obvious enjoyment of the massage pleased him. "I haven't stopped, I'm just moving to a new area."

He looked at her shirt and noticed, for the first time, that the writing on it was actually the signatures of her students, the names faded almost into oblivion by repeated washings. Mary, Tracy, Scott, Steve, Jason, Aaron, Jamie—he knew if he asked her, she'd be able to tell him about every one of them. Doubtless, Mary, Tracy, Scott and the others would have fond memories of Miss O'Leary, as well. She was that kind of teacher.

Grabbing the tail of the shirt, he pushed it up under her arms, baring her back. It was no more than he would see if she were wearing a swimsuit, but it seemed more intimate because they'd been lovers. And because he wanted to make love to her again. He picked up the lotion. "Get ready."

She gasped as he drizzled the cold liquid along her spine and then exhaled ecstatically as he spread it with his palms, smearing it to her shoulders and out over her ribs in firm, soothing strokes. He could see only the thinnest crescent of the side of her breast, but he was aware that her breasts were only inches from his fingertips, warm, soft, sensitive to his touch. He had only to slide his hand a bit farther around, a bit higher—

He resisted, kneading only the muscles crisscrossing her back and stretching over her ribs, while he listened to her breathless little moans of contentment and slowly went out of his mind wanting her. He worked his way down her spine to the small of her back, and drew tiny circles with his fingertips until she shifted restlessly.

"Undo the waistband of your shorts," he said.

"What?"

"We've taken care of the steering muscles, now we have to pay attention to the ones you sat on." He landed a swat on her backside for emphasis.

Arching, she unbuttoned her shorts.

"Cold lotion!" he warned, squeezing a strip of the peach-scented liquid in a line across her waist.

"Beast," she said. "You enjoy that too much."

"Not nearly as much as I enjoy rubbing it in," he said. "After tonight, I may never think of peaches quite the same way again." His hands moved in slow circles over her smooth, firm flesh, pushing the loosened waistband ever lower...

Erica's eyes were closed, her breathing shallow. This was no longer a simple back rub; it had ceased to be that when he'd moved below her waist. He was no hourly masseur performing his duties with professional detachment. This was Sean, her lover; Sean's hands on her buttocks, rubbing away the soreness of too many hours in the driver's seat, giving her not only relief, but pleasure; not just easing sore muscles, but arousing her. "Do you know what you're doing to me?" she asked.

"The same thing you're doing to me, I hope," he said, leaning forward to sweep his hands over her ribs and up, caressing her breasts. Erica inhaled sharply as tremors of arousal wracked her body.

She filled his senses; her beauty, the scent of the lotion, the velvety texture of her skin as he savored the plumpness of her breasts beneath his palms. She rolled over to face him, lifting her arms to rest her wrists on his shoulders, and locking her gaze with his, revealing the same consuming fascination for the magic drawing them together. "I'm glad you came tonight."

"I couldn't stay away knowing you were so close by."

Their mouths met tentatively, then fused urgently. Had it been only weeks since they'd been close like this? It seemed like forever. Impatient for the feel of his body against hers, Erica pulled away from him, yanked her shirt over her head, slipped off her shorts and tossed the garments aside. Then they both tore at Sean's clothes, fighting buttons, belts and zipper until shirt, pants and tie also lay in crumpled heaps on the floor.

Already aroused by the sensuous massage, Erica wrapped her arms around his neck and fell back on the sofa, pulling him with her. They kissed deeply, groping and kneading with breathless desire as gravity pressed their naked bodies together. Ultimately they coupled with the passion of lovers who were still new to each other, the familiarity of soul mates and the fury of two people desperate to be a part of each other until they appeased the unbearable need that drove them.

In the afterglow of their lovemaking, Erica stretched out full length atop Sean, stacking her hands on his chest and her chin on her hands so she could see his face. Her chuckle vibrated through both of them.

"What's so funny?" Sean asked.

"I was just thinking that if dead people really look down to watch over the people they love, then Gram must be scandalized by what we just did on her couch."

"Don't underestimate your grandmother," Sean said. "She might find our lack of discretion distasteful, but I doubt she would shock as easily as you think."

"You're probably right," Erica said, smiling softly. "You see her as a person. I'm still thinking of her as a grandmother."

"How is it, being back in her house?"

"Strange," she said. "I know she's gone, but I keep expecting—"

"To turn around and see her?"

"Yes," she said. "I know it sounds crazy, but everything is so familiar. It just seems impossible that she's not here."

"It's not crazy. It's not even unusual. It's perfectly normal."

"It's comforting being here, in a way—like having her close by." The thought faded into a sigh. "I'm still not looking forward to going through all her things, but I'll manage."

"Don't push yourself," he said. "There's no hurry."

"Summers have a way of flying by."

She felt him tense. "Do you really think I'm going to let you leave at the end of the summer?"

"We'll worry about that at the end of the summer," she said. No matter how mellow she was feeling right now, it was too soon for promises. "Tonight, we worry about tonight."

"Tonight, I'm the one who has to leave."

"As if I'd let you," she said, wriggling her breasts seductively against his chest.

His frown registered genuine reluctance. "I have to, Erica. I have a meeting first thing in the morning, and I have to go over some material tonight to prepare. As it is, I'll be up past midnight."

"You work too hard, O'Leary."

"I'm an attorney," he said. "We're all materialistic workaholics."

"You had to remind me," she said, scowling playfully. "And now I guess you're going to tell me you have to leave this very minute."

"I think I could *work* in a kiss before I go."

"No way!" Erica teased, arching her head out of his reach. "I know how you lawyers operate. If you *work me in*, I'll get billed for the extra time."

"This one's strictly *pro bono*."

"*Pro* whose *bono?*" she challenged.

"Mine," he said, guiding her face to his.

Once again, he showed his almost eerie ability to read her mood and respond to it. He kept the kiss gentle and unhurried, complementing the mellow afterglow instead of shattering it. The very gentleness of it swept over Erica's senses like an ocean wave, etching its memory on her heart and soul as surely as waves rippled sand.

At the door, she savored his sweet smile as he told her good-night one last time, then she waited until she heard him drive away before bolting the security locks. The new locks were the only things in the house lacking the patina of familiarity, but even as she resented the need for them, she appreciated the fact that they were there.

Turning off lights along the way, she went to the bedroom her grandmother had always maintained for her. The room had been her mother's when her mother was growing up, and although Erica had no conscious memories of her, she had fabricated elaborate fantasies about her as she'd played with the dolls and plastic horses and china tea sets that had belonged to her.

In later years, her elaborate fantasies had turned to daydreams and speculation about what her mother had been like and an awareness that her long-deceased mother had primped in the same mirror, looked out the same window, kept her clothes in the same drawers, slept in the same bed. Sometimes she'd lain in bed wondering what it must have been like to be Gram's daughter instead of her granddaughter; to be an only child, with a doting mother, instead of a motherless girl with a father whose pride was more important than his common sense, two stepmothers with no particular interest in her and two sets of step-siblings who made her feel like the eternal outsider.

Tonight as she climbed into the beautiful old bed, she was joined by Aunt Pitty-Pat, who meowed obnoxiously until Erica petted her. Then, in keeping with their nightly routine, the cat sprawled on her back, purring, while Erica rubbed the animal's chest vigorously. "Well, I had my rubdown, I guess you're entitled to one, too," Erica said. "And you know something, Pitty-Pat? Until tonight, I'd never realized how wonderful a good rubdown could be."

Aunt Pitty-Pat flipped onto her side so Erica could stroke her in long, shoulder-to-tail strokes. Soon the cat was sound asleep. Erica exhaled a heavy sigh as exhaustion from the long trip and the utter satisfaction of having been pampered and made love to by a good man took their toll in the quiet darkness.

"No offense, Pitty-Pat," she murmured on the edge of sleep, "but you're a poor substitute for a certain lawyer I know."

She slept until ten o'clock the next morning and, after the late start, the day flew by. She went grocery shopping, called the newspaper to have delivery started and unpacked the boxes of miscellaneous items she'd brought, finding niches for the special gifts made for her by her students. The teddy bear she'd had since childhood took his place on the pillows of her bed, along with the stuffed pig Sean had given her.

Her flip file of phone numbers and addresses went next to the phone, her aerobics dance tape in the rack next to the television. She was adding her own compact discs to her grandmother's extensive collection of classicals and sound tracks when Ardeth Maxwell yoo-hooed at the back door with a basket of muffins and a tin of herb tea. Erica put water on to boil, and she and Ardeth sat down at the kitchen table to chat.

"Have you decided what you're going to do about the house?" Ardeth asked.

Erica shook her head. "For now, I just want to go through everything. Maybe by the end of the summer I'll be able to decide whether to put it on the market or lease it out."

"Then you're definitely planning to go back to Georgia at the end of the summer?" Ardeth asked. "I thought maybe you'd decide to stay here."

"My job is in Georgia," Erica said as she poured two cups of tea and handed one to Ardeth. *Assuming she decided to keep it.* She had some tough decisions to make in the coming weeks.

"There are schools right here in Towson," Ardeth said. "Julia Hammer—you know Judith, don't you? She's one of the original Green Thumbs. Judith's a retired teacher, and her son is an administrator with the local district. I'll bet he'd set up interviews for you if you asked."

Erica smiled. "I'll keep that in mind if I decide to stick around."

Do you really think I'm going to let you leave? Sean's words played through her mind as she sipped her tea. But it was too soon to be building her life around a man she hardly knew.

Hardly knew? How could she hardly know a man who'd touched her very soul on the first night they'd met? A man who'd flown such a long way just to wish her happy birthday? A man who'd given her a back rub? A man who'd taken in her grandmother's cat?

"Goodness!" Ardeth said as Aunt Pitty-Pat sauntered into the kitchen, meowed disdainfully, then sat down and gave them a down-the-nose feline stare. "That's not Esmerelda."

"It's my cat, Aunt Pitty-Pat," Erica said. "Mr. O'Leary's going to keep Esmerelda a few more days while Aunt Pitty-Pat gets used to the house."

"Ah, yes. Mr. O'Leary." Ardeth took a sip and then placed her cup back in the saucer. "Isn't it the strangest coincidence, that lawyer's name being the same as yours?"

"O'Leary's not an uncommon name," Erica said. "There are plenty of Irish attorneys. I was on a whole train filled with them once."

"That must have been an adventure."

"More than you know," Erica said, remembering the feel of Sean's arms around her.

"That sounds like there's a story attached," Ardeth said shrewdly.

Erica waved away the woman's interest with a flap of her hand. "Not really. They were all partying, but I wasn't in the mood." She took a sip of tea. "It was when I was rushing here when Gram was ill."

"I can see how that could be disconcerting."

"Yes," Erica said, nodding. "Yes, it was. I felt very...alone." *Until Sean O'Leary put his arms around me and held me close.*

"It's a shame you had to make that trip by yourself."

"It's history now," Erica said. "And speaking of history and trips, I want to hear all about your tour of the Holy Land."

They talked for a half hour, then Erica walked through the greenhouse with Ardeth while the older woman attended to the seedlings she was starting for a fall garden.

After Ardeth left, Erica returned to the house, finished putting her CDs away and jotted some I-made-it-in-one-piece notes to her friends in Georgia. By the time she'd addressed the last letter, it was past four. She decided to do her nails—fingers and toes—in time for the polish to dry before she dressed for her date.

An hour later, she'd just immersed herself in scented bathwater and spread a mud-and-oatmeal facial on her face, when the phone rang. She got out of the tub, grabbed a towel and dashed for the phone, thinking that if it was a salesman, she'd climb through the lines and inflict bodily harm.

It was Sean, sounding harried. "Something's come up."

Erica's heart sank. *He was breaking their date.*

"I really want to see you," he continued. "Could we possibly go at six instead of eight? You can dress casual."

"Six? That's only—" *Half an hour!* She sighed wearily. "My hair is wringing wet."

"Six-thirty?"

She wanted to see him, too. "I won't be as stunning as I would be at eight."

"You'll be stunning." The sincerity with which he imbued the simple affirmation turned Erica's heart to mush. Whether or not she believed she was stunning, *he* would believe it.

After a beat of silence, he said her name.

"Um?" Erica's fingers tightened around the receiver as she waited for him to go on.

Finally, he said, "Last night was—"

Erica closed her eyes. A smile played at the edges of her mouth as she recalled the magic of his touch, the deep affection in his eyes. "Yes," she said. "It was."

Another interval passed in silence, mellowed by shared memories. At last, he said awkwardly, "Dress casual."

"My O'Leary's Porkers shirt is clean."

"Not that casual," he said, as though not quite certain that she was teasing. "This is Maryland, you know."

"It's not too stained," she pressed. "Most of the slime came out."

"It won't be the evening I'd planned, but I'll do better than a hamburger stand," he said grimly. "I . . . my house-keeper—"

"Your housekeeper? Don't tell me she forgot to do laundry again and you don't have any clean dress shirts."

She could hear his frustration as he exhaled on the other end of the line. "I'll explain everything when I get there."

After hanging up the phone, Erica, still holding the towel around her, sat on the corner of the bed mulling over the perplexing conversation. They weren't going to have their evening on the town as planned. That was disappointing, but it was hardly enough to produce the level of frustration she'd heard in Sean's voice. Maybe he was a control freak who didn't like any plan running amok, but nothing in his personality had ever suggested that kind of rigidity.

What could have shaken an ordinarily competent, easy-going man so much? Maybe the problem had him in a state of anxiety. Perhaps it was something related to his work. A difficult legal tangle, or a contested will. But he'd mentioned his housekeeper.

Her face crinkled in concentration. What could his house-keeper have done to vex him that way? Quit? Refused to do the windows? Maybe he was having an affair with her, and she'd found out he'd been with another woman and had ripped through his closet with a carving knife in a fit of jealous rage.

Why don't you think up some more outlandish scenarios, she chided herself. *An overactive imagination is such a terrible thing to waste!* With a sniff of exasperation, she rose and walked back to the bathroom to hurry through her bath—and wash away the facial pack that had dried so tightly it was putting pressure on her brain.

She rushed through hair and makeup before putting on a loosely pleated calf-length tan skirt and ecru shirt. At least she'd already polished her toenails when he'd called to move up the time of their date, she thought, wiggling her toes inside the sandalfoot stockings before slipping on leather sandals. As she tied the long, skinny straps of the sandals into bows in front of her ankles, she heard Sean's car pull into the driveway. The doorbell sounded as she walked from the bedroom to the living room.

Sean kissed her on the cheek as he entered the house, then self-consciously tucked his hands into the pockets of his khaki jeans and gave her a head-to-toe once-over. "You look . . . stunning."

"So do you," she replied, chancing a smile. "I like your shirt." It was a smart plaid with a button-down collar.

"Thanks," he said. "It was a Christmas present."

"Do you want to talk a while, have something to drink?"

He shook his head. "No. We have to—"

He was having too much trouble with simple words. Erica's scalp prickled. "What's going on, Sean?" she asked quietly.

"My housekeeper's mother had a stroke and she had to rush up to Trenton to see about her."

"What has that got to do with us tonight?" she asked. "I mean, do you need to stay at home and do laundry or something?"

Sean ran his right hand through his hair. "Of course not. I just . . . I tried, but I couldn't find—"

"Find what?" *Your clothes? Your car keys?*

Sean exhaled in a rush. "I couldn't find a baby-sitter."

Erica felt as though she'd had the wind knocked out of her. "A what?" *Had he said baby-sitter?*

"My children are in the car, Erica."

9

"CHILDREN?" *Children?* Erica struggled to absorb what he'd said. "You have children?"

Sean nodded.

"How many?"

"Two."

"They live with you?"

"Yes."

"All the time? You're the full-time custodial parent?"

"Yes."

"But you've never mentioned...all the times we've talked, you've never—" She glared at him accusingly. "Why?"

"This isn't the way I wanted to tell you."

Erica's shoulders sagged with the force of a weary sigh. "Never mind *how,* exactly *when* were you going to tell me?"

"Tonight. Over dinner, when we had privacy and time." He frowned. "Neither of which we have at the moment." He tilted his head toward the door. "They're outside in the car. Ready to meet them?"

His kids. She was going to meet his kids. Kids who lived with him. Kids she hadn't even known he had.

Slowly, she followed him outside. He opened the front passenger door and poked his head in the car, addressing the children in the back seat. "Michael. Kaitlin. This is the lady I told you about, Miss O'Leary. Erica, these are my children."

Erica leaned over the seat to look at the children as she told them hello, called each by name and asked their ages. Michael, a miniature Sean with an impish expression in his eyes that suggested he was plotting mayhem and mischief, informed her he was seven but he would be eight in three weeks.

Kaitlin also bore a strong resemblance to her father, but her features were softer. Her long, golden hair was pulled back into a barrette at her crown and wispy tendrils curled around her face. "I'm six years old," she said. "My teacher said I should be an artist because I'm a good drawer."

"Teachers are dumb," Michael said.

"Michael!" Sean warned. *Of all things for him to come out with.*

"Mrs. Duke said the Hubble found two new moons on Saturn, but they weren't really moons," Michael persisted. "They were just space stuff."

"Mrs. Duke just didn't hear the updated analysis of the original data," Sean said. His eyes cut to Erica. "But Michael enlightened her."

"I'll bet you just finished second grade, didn't you, Michael," Erica said.

"I'm in third grade now." Michael said.

"I teach third grade," Erica said.

"You're not going to be *my* teacher, are you?"

"No. I live in Georgia."

After she'd answered a few more of the children's questions, Erica got into the passenger seat, while Sean settled behind the steering wheel and started the engine.

"Can we have pizza?" Michael asked as Sean backed the sedan out of the driveway.

"No," Sean said. "We are not going to get pizza. We're not going to get hamburgers, either. We're going somewhere with real plates, and people who bring you food and fill your water glasses."

"Bummer!" Michael said disgustedly. "I like pizza."

"What's the name of the place that we're going to?" Kaitlin asked.

"I think we should let Miss O'Leary decide because she's our special guest," Sean said. He cocked an eyebrow. "Where to, Miss O'Leary?"

Erica thought a moment. "There's a little place called Verdi's off York Road that has wonderful fettuccine Alfredo."

"Fettuccine al barfo," Michael grumbled.

"Pretend you're in your room and take a time-out until the car stops, Michael," Sean said brusquely, adding under his breath to Erica, "He's having a bit of a memory problem—he's forgotten his manners."

"He's a seven-year-old boy," Erica replied in a confidential tone. "They don't acknowledge manners."

"They're all that way?" Sean asked.

"Ninety-nine percent of them."

"That's a relief. I thought I was raising a sociopath."

The hostess who seated them at the restaurant gave Sean and Erica menus and promised the children that the server would be with them shortly with children's coloring menus and crayons.

"Crayons!" Kaitlin exclaimed.

"Maybe you could draw a picture for my refrigerator," Erica said. "I don't have a thing on it right now."

"Our 'frigerator is *covered* with pictures," Kaitlin said. "Mrs. Smead puts all our papers on there."

"Mrs. Smead?" Erica asked, knowing the answer.

"She's our housekeeper. She takes care of us when Daddy's at work," Kaitlin said.

"She's mean," Michael said. "She makes us clean our rooms every Wednesday, and we have to put the sheets in the washer and measure the soap."

"When you grow up and live on your own, you'll know how to do laundry," Erica said.

Michael harrumphed. "When I grow up, I'll hire a housekeeper who's not too lazy to do the laundry like she's supposed to."

Frowning, Sean said, "I think we know who the lazy person in our house is."

Kaitlin giggled. "It's Michael! Michael's lazy."

"You two behave," Sean warned parentally as Michael scowled darkly at his sister. When the dark-haired young waitress arrived, putting a paper place mat and a handful of crayons in front of each child, he smiled gratefully. "Perfect timing."

Sean leaned over to read Kaitlin's menu, then looked at Erica. "I've been set up, haven't I?"

Erica grinned. "Just a little bit. Their fettuccine Alfredo *is* wonderful."

Sean looked at the server. "Two Alfredos and—" Turning to Kaitlin, he asked, "Smiley-face pizza or curly spaghetti?"

"Pizza!" the children replied in unison.

"You heard them," Sean said. "And bring the lady and me a carafe of—" he looked at Erica and lifted an eyebrow questioningly "—white wine?"

Erica nodded. After what he'd just sprung on her, she could use a stiff drink—which, with Erica's drinking habits, amounted to a glass of wine. Seeing attorney Sean O'Leary in daddy mode took a certain getting used to, especially since he'd never bothered to mention that he was a father.

"Coloring is for little kids," Michael said, pointedly avoiding picking up the crayons.

"There are word games and puzzles on the other side," the server said.

Erica took a pen from her purse and gave it to the boy. "Here you go."

As Michael began hunting for words in a word-search puzzle, Erica felt a definite tap of a foot against her own. She looked at Sean and discovered him staring at her. Their gazes locked, and the questions she desperately wanted to ask were on the tip of her tongue. But she could not ask them in front of the children. *Sean's* children.

"We'll talk later," he mouthed.

Why haven't we talked about your children before? She sucked in a ragged breath to keep from screaming the question. She'd felt so close to him, thought she knew him. They'd been lovers.

What else didn't she know? The question plagued her throughout the evening, despite Sean's efforts to make everything seem perfectly normal. She could not look at him without suffering conflicting emotions. Just last night he'd been her lover, tender and caring, but he had concealed a basic truth about himself. He had deceived her; if not by overt untruths, at least by omission.

The server returned with the carafe of wine. Erica gratefully sipped hers, using it as a means of avoiding conversation. She didn't feel like making small talk, pretending everything was all right.

A gentle scrape on her arm drew her attention to Kaitlin, who was poking her with the edge of her place mat. "This is for your 'frigerator," the child said. "I wrote your name on it. See? Miss O'Leary."

"Yes, I see. And you spelled it correctly."

"O'Leary is my name, too."

Erica smiled. "I guess that makes both of us Miss O'Leary."

"Aunt Kathy's name was Miss O'Leary before she married Uncle Bob," Kaitlin said.

"How many Miss O'Learys does that make?" Erica asked.

Kaitlin's face screwed up in concentration for a moment before she answered, "Three."

"You're a very clever girl, Kaitlin," Erica said. *And very adorable.* It would be very easy to become attached to her. And to her grumpy older brother, for that matter. Michael was so typically seven-almost-eight, and he looked so much like Sean. *Why, Sean?* she thought as her heart broke. *Why?*

"Oooo," Michael mocked. "She can count to three. She must be a genius."

Sean shot the boy a quelling look and tried to change the subject before a fight broke out. "Hey, guys, Miss O'Leary is the lady we've been keeping Esmerelda for."

Erica suspected that Sean probably hadn't anticipated the reaction he got to his revelation. Narrowing his eyes, Michael glared at Erica and challenged, "Are you going to make us give her back?"

"Esmerelda was Miss O'Leary's grandmother's cat," Sean said patiently. "Of course Miss O'Leary wants her back."

Kaitlin, her countenance suddenly tragically crestfallen, said, "We love Esmerelda. We don't want her to go away."

Sean's frustration was exceeded only by his embarrassment. *What had gotten into his children? Why had they picked tonight of all nights to get weird? Insulting teachers, making Erica seem like a meanie for reclaiming her own cat— no telling what they would come up with next.*

Kaitlin—dear, sweet Kaitlin—turned to Erica and asked softly, "Why did your grandmother send Esmerelda away? Doesn't she love her anymore?"

"My grandmother died," Erica replied, surprised that she could say it so easily.

"Is she in heaven with our mother?" Kaitlin asked.

Something like an electrical shock quivered up Erica's spine, and from the heat she felt in her face, she was certain it was bright red. But no redder than Sean's was pale as their gazes locked across the table. *It was true. His wife was dead, and he'd told her—*

No. That wasn't true. He hadn't told her he was divorced, but he'd let her believe it.

He'd let her believe it!

"Y-yes," she told Kaitlin. "My grandmother's in heaven."

"If she's in heaven, then why does she still need a cat?"

"That is enough!" Sean snapped. "You've known from the beginning that Esmerelda was only going to be with us a short while."

A pall fell over the table, and for a long moment it seemed as if no one would ever speak again after Sean's uncharacteristic outburst. Erica found herself choking back a sob. *Poor little Kaitlin,* Erica thought. *She was so sincere.*

Sean prepared to speak, but Erica shook her head and forced a smile as she addressed the children, "I'll bet you've been taking really good care of Esmerelda."

The children nodded. Erica swallowed hard, and drew in a deep breath. "I think my grandmother would be pleased to know Esmerelda has people who love her. If it's all right with your father, she can be your kitty now."

The children turned to Sean, regarding him with the wide-eyed anticipation of baby birds waiting on a worm. "Please, Daddy?"

Sean rolled his eyes. "How could I possibly say no?" He grinned at Erica. "Of course, Miss O'Leary will have to come visit her from time to time."

Erica responded by taking another sip of wine. She made it through the meal and the ride back to her house by focusing primarily on the children, talking to them about Esmerelda, school, pizza, Cub Scouts, spaceships and Miss Piggy. Before leaving the car, she got a hug from Kaitlin as she thanked the little girl for the refrigerator art and even a grudging grin from Michael as she asked him to take good care of Esmerelda.

As Sean walked her up to her front door, all she could think of was getting inside the house where she could be alone, with the space and privacy to think. Perversely, her key refused to work in the lock. She exhaled an exasperated growl.

"Trouble?" Sean asked.

"This new lock. I think Gary put it on a little crooked."

"Here. Let me try." His after-shave set off a dizzying set of sensual memories as he stepped next to her and reached for the key. "Sometimes if you apply a little body language—" He pulled up and jiggled at the same time and the lock yielded with a click. He opened the door, extracted the key and handed it to her.

"Thank you," she said. "And . . . thank you for dinner."

His expression grim, he studied her face for a long time before speaking. "It rips my heart apart when you talk to me that way."

"W-what way?" she asked, swallowing uncomfortably.

"As though we're polite strangers. Or adversaries forced to go through the motions of being polite."

"Are you sure that's not what we are?" she asked, struggling for composure.

"Which do you mean—strangers or adversaries?"

"Maybe both," she said. "You're an attorney and, tonight, I found out you're also a stranger."

"I'm *your* attorney. That makes me an advocate, not an adversary. And I'm certainly no stranger to you."

"You're certainly not the man I knew—or thought I knew."

"Because I have children?" He put his hands on her shoulders but she shrugged them away, turning her back to him.

"Because you weren't honest with me," she said. She turned around to face him with accusation in her eyes. "I'm not naive enough to expect forever just because I go to bed with a man, but there are certain reasonable assumptions a woman is entitled to make about the man she's sleeping with. One of them is honesty."

"I never lied to you."

"You're a widower?"

"Yes."

"I thought you were divorced."

"I never told you that. You *assumed* it."

"You never corrected me."

"You asked if I had a wife, and I said no. You never asked if I had children."

"That's attorney double-talk," she said. "Whatever happened to 'the truth, the whole truth, and nothing but'?"

"This is life, Erica, not a 'Perry Mason' rerun."

"Thank you for clarifying that! Now I know better than to expect ethical behavior from an attorney. That only happens in fiction." *She wouldn't be counting on any happy endings, either.*

"This has nothing to do with my being an attorney, Erica. My children are vulnerable. I have a responsibility to protect them."

"From me?" she asked incredulously.

"From getting attached to you and then—"

"I see." *All too clearly.*

"I don't think you do. You think I took a chance when I got on that plane and flew to Georgia for your birthday? That was peanuts compared to the chance I took tonight. If my date had been with anyone else, I would have canceled it instead of bringing the children along."

"It's not that you didn't take me home to meet the kiddies, Sean. It's that you didn't trust me enough to tell me about them." Erica released a resigned sigh. "I can't help wondering what else you're not telling me."

"There's very little about me you don't know at this point," Sean said. "I'm an attorney with a thriving practice and I'm also a single parent. Even if I wanted some dark, secret life, I wouldn't have time for it." He sighed wearily. "It's useless to try to have this conversation when the kids are waiting in the car."

She turned her back to him again. "I'm not much in the mood for conversation right now, anyway."

"How upset are you?" he asked softly.

She answered with a shrug and a sniff.

"As bad as that?"

"Worse!" she snapped petulantly.

He cupped her shoulders again and, this time, she didn't pull away. Nor did she turn into his embrace, although she longed to. She stood motionless as he leaned over her right shoulder to kiss her cheek and whisper good-night.

As soon as he was out the door, she changed into her bed clothes and curled into her favorite overstuffed armchair to watch a prime-time hospital drama. The show would not start for a few minutes, so she muted the sound. Drawing her legs up, she propped her chin on her knees and sighed. She couldn't believe Sean had been callous enough to conceal the fact that he had children. And to let her believe that he was divorced when, in fact, he was a widower. *What had happened to his wife? How had she died?*

She disgustedly mimicked his words aloud. "You asked if I had a wife, and I said no. You never asked if I had children." She picked up a throw pillow and hurled it across the room. "I didn't ask if you had any contagious diseases, but I would have expected you to mention it if you had!"

No matter how long she mulled over the situation, her conclusion regarding his penchant for withholding personal information was going to be the same: he was deceitful. And she wasn't sure which disturbed her most—the fact that he was deceitful, or the equally abhorrent fact that she had been so wrong about him. She had let vulnerability cloud her judgment when she was troubled and feeling alone or over-whelmed. She'd overcome her well-founded prejudice against attorneys and looked past what he did for a living, thinking she'd found a decent man, only to discover that he was as wily and unprincipled as every lawyer she'd ever encountered.

Oh, how she loathed the arrogance with which attorneys played with the truth! Truth, to Sean O'Leary, as to all the attorneys she'd dealt with, was selective; a tool to be used or withheld, or blended with innuendo to advantage, a toy to play with, stretching, shaping and pinching like a child working a clump of clay.

The story line of the hospital show involved a doctor accused of malpractice in the unavoidable death of a patient. The moment the screen filled with lawyers sitting around a table discussing defense strategy, Erica switched channels, but the focus of the prime-time newsmagazine she'd turned to was on the ethics of the insanity defense. She changed channels again, but the movie on the last major network was a court-room drama based on a bestselling suspense novel by an attorney. Disgusted, Erica turned off the television and flung the remote control onto the sofa. Damn lawyers—wasn't it enough to destroy lives in reality—did they have to monopolize the airways, too?

Deciding to hit the sack early, she went to the bathroom to prepare for bed. She was brushing her teeth as though world peace depended on the removal of plaque, when the phone rang.

Sean O'Leary, no doubt. She froze a moment, listening to the persistent ringing as she debated whether or not to answer it. She wished she'd had the good sense to turn on the answering machine on her way to the bathroom.

Slurping water, she rinsed quickly and dashed to the phone. She could hear his impatience in the persistent way the bell sounded; she might as well talk to him and get it over with. It wasn't as though she was going to get any sleep tonight, anyway.

"Hello," she barked with all the warmth of a general issuing an order.

"I was getting worried because you didn't answer."

"What's wrong, Counselor? Did you think I was so distraught that I was out in some sleazy club sobbing into a warm beer?"

"You're still upset, I take it."

"I'm . . . disheartened," she said, her tone of voice carrying the message as emphatically as the actual words.

"My sister just called," he said. "I'd left a message on her machine when I was hunting for a baby-sitter. She and her family just got back from a birthday dinner for her father-in-law. She said she'd come to my house for a while if I need her. I'd like to see you, Erica."

"That wouldn't be a good idea. I'm already undressed."

"I don't mind." His voice was sultry and suggestive.

Erica gripped the receiver so tightly her knuckles turned white. "Please don't, Sean."

"What's it going to take, Erica?"

That's it—negotiate like a proper lawyer. Find out what I want and then plot out some cagey strategy. "I thought you were different!" she snapped.

"Different from what?"

"From every attorney I've ever met!"

She sensed his frustration in the silence that followed. "At least let me come over so we can talk this through face-to-face," he said.

"Talking isn't going to fix anything," she replied, aching with the conviction of her words. "This is one situation you can't negotiate yourself out of, Counselor."

"Ever?" Sean challenged. Her intractable attitude was beginning to chafe at him.

She deliberated a while before replying, "I don't know. I need some time—" She exhaled heavily. "Maybe when I come to your office to sign those papers next week—"

"You can't be ready to throw away our relationship over something as trivial as how or when I told you I had children," Sean said incredulously. *Didn't she realize what was at stake?*

"Only a lawyer would consider honesty between lovers a trivial issue."

"My being a lawyer has nothing to do with our personal relationship," he said. "We're talking about bad timing, not deception."

"That's a distinction only a lawyer would make."

Sean fought to keep his temper in check. "Damn it, Erica! This is a personal matter between the two of us, not a legal one. This has nothing to do with my being an attorney."

"It has to do with honesty and ethics, and lawyers seem to have their own definitions for those good old-fashioned values."

"This is asinine, Erica. You're creating an issue where it doesn't exist. I made an error in judgment, for which I'm ready to explain and apologize but, frankly, I'm getting tired of defending my profession to you. I know it's fashionable to hold lawyers in contempt. I've heard the lawyer jokes. But as long as there have been laws, there have been lawyers to interpret and defend them."

"And at least as far back as Shakespeare, the idea of killing all the lawyers has appealed to a certain segment of society."

"Several segments, actually—anarchists, tyrants and political rebels intent on creating chaos and overthrowing governments—"

"People who've been screwed in divorce wars," she countered. "Businesses that have paid out millions of dollars in judgments to people who injured themselves while blatantly misusing a product, anyone who's fallen victim to some frivolous suit brought by some greedy litigant intent on exploiting the system—"

Sean's jaw clenched as he listened to her tirade. "This conversation is going nowhere."

"At least we agree on that," she said.

Dead silence followed. Sean swallowed. "Erica—"

"Good night, O'Leary," she said with an unmistakable note of finality.

"I hope to God you never need an attorney for anything beyond routine paperwork, but if you ever do, I guarantee you'll be damned glad to see one!"

"And pigs fly!"

The connection ended with an abrupt click. Stunned, Sean held the receiver for a full two minutes before redialing her number. He let it ring ten times before hanging up.

Pigs *would* fly before he dialed that number again. What had he done, anyway? Just tried to protect his children. He'd been planning to tell her about them when he was in Georgia, but everything had gotten—

She'd been so tacky in that field-day shirt smeared with slime—tacky, grubby and completely irresistible. He'd known from the sparkle in her eyes when she first saw him that she was glad he'd come, and after that—well, he'd given her the bracelet and there had been dinner. The subject of his children hadn't seemed appropriate. Their time together had been private and enchanted, just for the two of them.

And last night, she'd been exhausted— *So cuddly in her comfortable clothes and dewy fresh from the shower. So female and . . . sexy.* The moment hadn't seemed right then, either.

He sighed wearily. He'd tried. He'd hit the redial button. She was the one who hadn't picked up the phone. He couldn't crawl through the line and make her talk to him. He'd have to give her some time to stew a bit and then try to patch things up with her.

Right now, he had to call his sister and tell her not to bother coming over. He wasn't going anywhere tonight—certainly not to visit Erica O'Leary.

10

CLIPBOARDS. Legal pads. Colored-dot labels. Erica carried the items to the cashier's booth at the office-supply store. She had dragged herself out of bed at first light after a sleepless night, determined to throw herself full force into the chore of sorting her grandmother's belongings. If the sheer volume of work involved didn't take her mind off Sean O'Leary, surely the inevitable emotional toll of going through her grandmother's things would.

Letting the phone ring last night had been one of the hardest things she'd ever done. She'd reached for it twice, and made herself hold back both times. What was the use of talking, when they had such opposite things to say? When they looked at everything from such diverse perspectives? It wasn't as though they were arguing over which team would win the pennant or which flavor of ice cream was best. They were at odds over basic issues of values and honesty.

Looking back on it, she was willing to concede that she might have overreacted a bit. And she might have gone a little overboard in her criticism of attorneys. Sean O'Leary couldn't be held accountable for the problems of the American justice system any more than she could for all the problems of the American educational system. He'd just punched the wrong button when he'd told her she'd be glad to see an attorney.

Glad to see an attorney? She'd rather face a hungry shark in rough seas!

Which was not to say that she wouldn't be glad to see a certain attorney named Sean O'Leary. How could she have been so lonely for him in the old four-poster bed when he'd never shared it with her? How could she ache for him when they'd made love just two nights ago? How could she feel as if a major chunk of her life had been snatched away, when they'd spent so little time together?

She knew the answer to the last question, at least. Every time she'd been with him, there had been an emotional-intensity factor that couldn't be translated into seconds, minutes and hours. She'd been distraught on the train when he'd comforted her; in a state of shock when they'd picnicked in the park; overwhelmed by the romance when he'd shown up for her birthday in Georgia.

And when he'd arrived unexpectedly to give her a back rub, she'd been just plain overwhelmed by *him*. He'd been a sensitive, caring, wildly romantic lover when they were together on her grandmother's couch—too bad he'd been hiding essential information about his personal life from her.

A widower. She found herself more curious about Sean's wife now that she knew the woman was dead than when she'd believed he was divorced. Ex-wives tended to lose halos in the divorce process; dead wives acquired them. Who was this woman he'd been married to? What had she been like? What had she looked like? What kind of mother had she been? What kind of wife? How had she died? And when?

"Are you ready to check out?"

Erica dropped her purchases on the counter. "Yes. Sorry," she told the cashier. "I must have been daydreaming."

"Aren't we all?" the cashier said. "It's too pretty to be indoors on a day like today. We should be down at the harbor instead of cooped up in here."

"You're right," Erica agreed. "You are absolutely right." What the hell—it *was* too pretty to be inside, and she deserved a break. She'd worked like a stevedore getting ready to move, while doing the end-of-school-year paperwork, and she had the whole summer ahead of her to go through her grandmother's house. She'd go down to the Inner Harbor and shop until she dropped. What good was being a multimillionairess if you couldn't enjoy a beautiful day occasionally?

The spontaneous outing proved therapeutic. At noon, having worked her way through half the shops at the Inner Harbor complex, she stopped at a waterside café for a leisurely lunch. After ordering crab cakes and salad, she took a moment to tuck several of the small plastic shopping bags she had accumulated on her spree into the largest. So many shops, so little time! Already she'd bought lobster refrigerator magnets for her friends in Georgia, a colorful sleepshirt, a pair of sandals, a comical lobster notepad and several rubber stamps. And she still had dozens of stores to explore.

One of the last shops she stopped in on her way out of the complex was an art store cleverly named Wings of Fantasy. The universal theme of the objets d'art within was wings. Angels, birds, mystical creatures took flight on the walls, on easels and pedestals and glass etagères, in prints and sculptures and collectible figurines. And there, framed in a gilt rococo frame, a tiny but exquisite oil painting caught her eye. She wanted it the instant her gaze settled on it. It was a fantasy creature with gossamer wings hovering near a cloud.

The fantasy creature was a pig, delicate, sweet and rosy-cheeked. Tears burned her eyes as she stared at the painting. "Oh, Sean," she whispered, "Pigs *do* fly."

Despite the outrageous price, Erica bought the postcard-size painting, along with an ornate tabletop easel on which to display it, then marveled at her impulsive action as she carried the fruits of her buying binge to the car.

Ardeth Maxwell's car was parked in front of the house when Erica arrived home, and Ardeth walked out of the greenhouse as Erica carried her purchases into the house.

"You've been shopping," she observed.

"I went to the Inner Harbor," Erica said. "If you have time for a cup of tea, I'll show you what I bought." Ardeth followed her into the kitchen. Erica put the bags on the table and filled the kettle. She showed the older woman the painting while the water heated. "It's silly, I know, but it just...spoke to me."

"That's the only true test of art," Ardeth said, stepping back and squinting as she studied the painting. "It speaks to me, too. It's . . . whimsical."

"Exactly," Erica said, jumping up as the kettle whistled. While the tea brewed, she located a bag containing several chunks of white chocolate fudge from a harbor *chocolatier* and offered one to Ardeth.

"I'm going to go through Gram's drawers and closet tomorrow," she said, taking a piece of the candy herself.

"Want some company?" Ardeth asked.

"I was hoping you'd offer," Erica answered. "You knew Gram so well. There may be some things that you'd like, or that you know one of her other friends would like."

Ardeth left as soon as she'd finished her tea, promising to return the following morning. Erica carried the fantasy pig to her bedroom to find a place for it. Displayed on the easel, it went perfectly atop the bedside console. *Where I'll be able to see it first thing in the morning and last thing at night*, she thought. *Just the perfect little masochistic reminder of Sean.*

Hoping against hope he had called her, she checked the answering machine, but there were no messages. She stared at the little red light, which perversely refused to blink, and wondered if she should call him. After all, she reasoned, she *had* overreacted, and he *had* called back. If she had answered the phone, they might have reached some tentative resolution already. On the other hand, he'd only tried to call back once, which means it could have been a coincidentally timed wrong number. Then again—

She glared at the phone. *Who was she trying to kid? She missed him so much her chest ached just thinking about him.* She would call Sean and apologize for overreacting. Then she'd see what happened from there.

She dialed his office number and got a recording saying that the office had closed for the day and emergency messages could be left with the answering service by dialing a separate number. Instead, she tried his home number and got a recording telling her to leave a message at the beep.

Frowning, she abandoned the whole idea and hung up without leaving a message, then sat down to write notes to her friends on the lobster notepaper. Hopefully, tomorrow she would be too busy sorting through her grandmother's belongings to fret about Sean.

THEY STARTED with the closet. Erica approached the meticulously ordered clothing on the rods of Gram's closet with sorrow. Her grandmother had grouped her wardrobe according to type—shirts, skirts, blouses, jackets, dresses, trousers. *Trousers*, Erica thought with a bittersweet smile. Her grandmother had never called them pants or slacks, only trousers.

"Are you sure you don't want to take some of the newer things to a consignment store?" Ardeth asked as Erica took an oxford-cloth shirt from a hanger to fold it and put it into a box.

"It would be a hassle. I'd rather give them away," Erica said. "I'm just glad you're doing the sorting. I wouldn't know what to send where."

"I've been volunteering at the thrift shop long enough to develop a sixth sense about what will fly and what won't."

Pigs fly, Erica thought, missing Sean.

When they'd finished the heart-wrenching task of going through the closet and drawers, Erica carried the boxes to Ardeth's car, and thanked the older woman profusely for her help. Returning to the house, she sat down to read the newspaper she'd abandoned upon Ardeth's arrival that morning.

Her thoughts soon strayed from the headlines she was reading to the man she was missing. Finally, with a groan of resignation, she phoned his office.

"Mr. O'Leary is in court this afternoon," the receptionist informed her. "May I take a message?"

"No, I—" She sighed deeply. "It's not an emergency. I'll be seeing Mr. O'Leary next week. I'll talk to him then."

She picked up the paper again, determined to read it this time. She paid particular attention to the real-estate listings, trying to get an idea what homes in the area were selling for. There weren't a lot of listings, but the few prices quoted were surprisingly high. Towson was a popular suburb with a patina of respectability, and the influx of picturesque office buildings and trendy shops had turned the postwar building-boom homes into figurative pots of gold because of their location. The houses might be old and their architectural style dated, but the land on which they were situated was prime real estate. If she put Gram's house on the market, she'd draw a good price.

But money wasn't the issue. She already had more money than she knew what to do with. She just hated the idea of giving up the house that was chock-full of her personal history. Her mother had grown up here, and for herself the house had been a refuge from the chaos that so often prevailed in her father's household.

She was more like Gram than she'd ever realized. The thought brought a smile to her face. She'd spent less than two hundred dollars yesterday, but had left the Inner Harbor feeling decadent and extravagant. She didn't want a lot from life—just meaningful work, the security of a roof over her head and—

Love. The same as Gram, she realized with a flash of insight. When Gram had fought for the right to be a part of her granddaughter's life, she'd been pursuing love. She had lost everything—her husband and child—and she had been clinging to her last connection to them. Erica bowed her head a moment, blinking back tears. *Oh, Gram. I'm so glad you didn't give up. I needed you so much.*

And what do you need now? she asked herself, tilting her head back and drawing in a deep breath. *You're all grown-up, and Gram's gone. What kind of love do you need?*

The answers were simple. She wanted a home, the kind of peaceful existence she'd been denied as a child. She wanted a man she could love and one who would love her. She wanted children—not just the students she cared about, but children of her own, children for whom she could make a home. She wanted to *belong.*

The faces of Michael and Kaitlin O'Leary came to mind, *Sean's children. The children he'd failed to tell her about.* She could love them so easily—

Why don't you just go write "Erica Loves Sean" on the sidewalk in front of his house? she thought disgustedly.

What was she doing sitting around pining for a man, anyway? She had *time* on her hands. *Leisure time.* The kind of leisure time she and her fellow teachers often dreamed of during hectic days of classes and tests, grading papers and keeping chattering, giggling, high-spirited children under control and motivated to learn. There were books to read, movies she'd wanted to see, visits she'd wanted to make to museums. How many years had it been since she'd been to the aquarium just to watch the fish swim? How long had it been since she'd taken a sketch pad and charcoal pencil into a park and tried to capture a scene for the sheer satisfaction of self-expression?

Time was too precious to waste sitting around yearning for an attorney she couldn't get in touch with. There was a library close by filled with books and a video-rental store next to the Chinese restaurant where she could get carry-out for dinner. Her decision was made.

By the time she went to all three places, the sunny day had given way to a cloudy dusk, and the temperature had dropped steadily since sunset. Erica shivered in the unseasonal cold as she crossed the small parking lot from the restaurant to her car.

Back at the house, she carried in the cartons of Chinese food and left them on the dining-room table while she went to her room to change from her soft-sleeved blouse into a sweatshirt and put on a pair of warm socks. She was comfortable, she had a good movie to watch and moo goo gai pan and fried rice.

Life was very nearly perfect.

Of course, she thought, glancing at the unblinking red eye of the answering machine, life would be even better if she'd come home to find a message from Sean. *Hello. Thinking of you. Miss you. Want you.*

Squaring her shoulders, she resolved not to think of him again for the rest of the evening. She turned on the television and switched it to the VCR channel, then realized that the library books she'd checked out and the videos she'd rented were still on the back seat of her car. Slipping a pair of slippers over her socks, she padded out to the car to get them.

The sky was cloudier than before, and the wind had picked up. Thinking that there must be a storm brewing, she quickly gathered the books and videos into her arms, shoved the door closed with her hip and started back to the house, hugging the small items closer to her body as another gust of wind threatened to blow them out of her grip.

She was actually looking at the front door of the house when it slammed shut with a crash as loud as a shotgun blast. Once over the shock of the noise, she froze, staring at the closed door as her jaw dropped in disbelief. Knowing the lock would have automatically engaged, she nevertheless put the books and videotapes on the doorstep and tried to turn the knob, jimmying it roughly when a gentle jiggle produced no results.

Dropping her hands to her sides, she rolled her eyes and groaned. This wasn't happening. It couldn't be. She refused to be locked out of her own house when she had Chinese food inside getting cold! She was supposed to be inside, devouring moo goo gai pan and Brad Pitt. She was supposed to be *relaxing*.

Stubbornly, she gave the doorknob one more savage twist, and then socked the door with her fist, growling a vile word she zealously reserved for only the worst of occasions. But all she got out of the gesture besides the noise was a sore hand.

There had to be a way to get inside, a window or door unlocked. She just had to find it. But even as she gave herself the pep talk, she knew she wasn't going to find any unlocked windows or doors. The doors locked automatically, and she was meticulous about locking the windows when she closed them. Still, she made a circuit of the house trying every one.

Her efforts were in vain. Back where she'd started, she released a sigh of resignation. What was she supposed to do now?

Groaning at her own obtuseness, she slapped her forehead. "Well, duh!" she said aloud. "Why don't you just go get the extra key the Winkles keep in the cookie jar on their kitchen counter, Miss O'Leary?"

Her grandmother and the Winkles had exchanged house keys for as long as Erica could remember. She'd even had an extra set of keys made for the Winkles when she purchased the new security locks.

In case she locked herself out. As much out of hysteria as self-deprecating amusement, Erica chuckled at the irony.

While she stood on the doorstep chuckling, her phone rang.

Once, twice, three times. Knowing the machine had answered the call, she pressed her ear to the door and strained to hear, but, except for the signal beep, everything else was muddled.

It could be Sean! she thought frantically.

It could be anyone who has your phone number. It could be a salesman. It could be a wrong number.

With a growl of frustration, she stalked off to the Winkles' house, gratefully noting the light in their living-room window. She rang the doorbell and waited, rang it a second time and waited, then beat on the door. Obviously the Winkles had gone out and left their lights on. Probably to make it appear as though they weren't out.

She'd just have to go inside and get the key herself. She tried the door and was not surprised to discover it locked. Undaunted, she walked around the house to the back door. It, too, was locked.

Erica scowled. The Winkles had certainly picked a rotten time to get meticulous about locking doors. What had happened to the quality of life in this town anyway? Erica could remember a time when no one in Towson locked their doors.

Still frowning, she went over to the nearest window and peered inside. The cookie jar was on the counter, within reach if she could only get the window open. Knowing Mrs. Win-

kle preferred fresh air to air-conditioning and so the window
might well be unlocked, Erica attempted to remove the screen
so she could try the window. It was firmly engaged.

Was everything *going to go wrong tonight?* she wondered
as she searched for something she could use as a wedge between the sill and the bottom of the screen. Luck, for once,
was on her side. Mrs. Winkle had left several garden tools in
a clay pot near the door. Mumbling about how crazy the
world had gotten, Erica selected a narrow, pointed spade,
forced the tip under the bottom edge of the screen and jiggled.

"Police officer. Don't make any sudden moves."

"What?" Erica asked incredulously, turning toward the
deep voice despite the stern admonition. About ten feet away
and walking toward her was a policeman about her age. He
was large—*very* large—and solidly built.

And he was aiming a gun at her.

"Drop your weapon, put your hands behind your head and
don't make any sudden moves," he ordered gruffly.

"Weapon?"

"Do it!"

Realizing he must mean the spade, Erica dropped it.

"Hands behind your head," the cop barked.

A loaded gun pointed at a person's chest was an excellent
persuader. Erica put her hands behind her head. "This must
look bad, but I can explain—"

"Are you alone?" the officer snapped.

Every muscle in his body—and he had plenty of them—
was tensed. *He's afraid of me,* Erica thought, astounded. *He's
afraid I have an accomplice.*

Great! Just great! The only thing worse than having a large
cop pointing a gun at you was having a large, *nervous* cop
pointing a gun at you. "Yes," she said. "I live next door and

I locked myself out and I came over to get the extra key the Winkles keep in their cookie jar."

"You'll have a chance to tell your story at the station."

"The station? I'm not a burglar."

"Keep your hands behind your head," he ordered.

She hadn't even realized she was lowering them. "It's awkward holding them up so high."

"I've called for backup," he said. "They should be here any time. When they do, we'll cuff you."

"Cuff me? But I'm not . . . I'm a schoolteacher!" she said, blurting out the first thing that popped into her head.

"What school?"

"Suwannee Elementary."

"There's no Suwannee Elementary in Towson."

"It's in Georgia."

"You said you lived next door."

"I do. I mean, my grandmother does. Did! She died two months ago. I inherited the house. I just moved here for the summer."

"Do you have any identification?"

Erica thought frantically. "Not on me. I just came outside to get a few things out of the car, and the wind blew the front door shut. It's an automatic lock." She brightened a bit. "The insurance and registration papers are in my glove compartment, but you'll have to break into my car." *Just her luck, she'd set it to lock when she'd opened the door to get the books and videos.*

"You want me to break into a car to look at the registration?"

"*My* car," she said. "It's right next door. You can call in the license plates and see. It's registered in my name, Erica Susan O'Leary."

The squeal of tires signaled the arrival of a second police car, and another officer, pushing forty and not quite as large, got out. "What have we here, Officer Harris?"

"Caught this little lady trying to break in. Says she lives next door and the wind blew her front door shut." The skeptical way he told it made the story sound ridiculous, even to Erica.

"The Winkles keep a spare key to my house in that cookie jar," she said, pointing to infuse her claim with some credibility.

"Right," the veteran cop said sarcastically. Stepping behind Erica, he grabbed the hand with which she'd just pointed and slapped a cuff on her wrist. He directed her arm behind her back, then guided her left wrist down close enough to the right to engage the second cuff.

"Ow," Erica said as the cuff pinched her flesh.

Ignoring her, the veteran addressed the younger officer. "Any ID?"

"Oh, I thought you'd never ask," he said, imitating the older officer's polished sarcastic style. "No ID, but she suggested I go next door and break into her car to check the registration."

"I thought you'd probably have one of those...*tools*," Erica said lamely.

"Sure. We break into cars all the time. They teach us how at the academy," the older cop said.

"She says she's a schoolteacher."

"I *am* a schoolteacher," Erica said. The younger cop was certainly braver now that he had another officer around to help bully her. At least he was holstering his gun. "I teach third grade."

"Way down upon the Suwannee River in Georgia," the big cop said.

"Well, do tell," the older cop said sarcastically. "Does the school board know what you do at night?"

"I was just going to watch a movie and eat Chinese food," Erica said dismally as the cop patted strategic areas to check for weapons. "Oh, for Pete's sake! I'm not armed!"

"Easy," the cop ordered. "You don't want to add resisting arrest to the list of charges."

"Charges?" Erica said, groaning dismally. "I told you, the Winkles keep a key to my house in their cookie jar. They gave me a key to their house, too, in case of emergency."

"Sure," the older cop said. "I don't know why we didn't see it right away—you have a key to their house, but you decided to put on dark clothing and break in through a window."

"Must be a new form of aerobics," the younger cop quipped.

"*Their* key is locked in my house, along with *my* key," Erica explained. "And this sweatshirt happened to be at the top of the drawer when I decided to put on a long-sleeved shirt. And I certainly wouldn't wear house slippers to go housebreaking."

"Wouldn't make much noise or leave much of a print," the older officer commented, eyeing the soft-fabric shoes. "And I suppose your neighbors' security system just slipped your mind."

"Security system?" she blurted out as the officer's words sank in.

"Oh, they forgot to tell you!" he said with mock empathy. He shook his head as though he couldn't believe her stupidity. "You've been lighting up all kinds of silent alarms down at the security-company monitoring office, lady."

"I don't believe this!" Erica said. She might as well have been talking to the wind whipping at her clothes and hair, because both the officers were looking at the street, where two more patrol units had pulled in with lights flashing.

"Here comes the cavalry," the older cop said. "You got a set of leg irons with you?"

"Leg irons?" Erica said.

"We wouldn't want you running off on us," the officer told her. "It might make us look bad."

The cops who'd just arrived joined them as the older policeman was putting the ankle cuff around her right ankle. One of them, a tall, rugged-looking man with graying dark hair and a ragged scar on his cheek eyed her from head to toe. "You've got to be kidding."

"That's what I said," Erica said, wincing as the second cuff clicked around her left ankle.

"It gets better," the veteran officer said. Then, as huge raindrops began falling, he cursed. "Let's get her into the station or we'll all be wringing wet."

Officer Harris nodded and wrapped huge fingers around her upper right arm. The older cop did the same on her left, and they walked her to the closest police car. Their progress was slow.

"Come on, speed it up," the veteran said. "We're getting wet here."

"I'm going as fast as I can," Erica said, feeling the first compulsion to cry. It was everything Erica could do to lift her feet with the constricting shackles. "I feel like Jacob Marley."

Both officers tensed. "Madman Marley?"

"Jacob Marley," Erica repeated. "*The Christmas Carol?* Charles Dickens?"

The older cop rolled his eyes. "Maybe she *is* a schoolteacher."

Erica had the horrible, almost surreal feeling that she was stuck in some cop-show episode as Officer Harris spread his hand on her head to prevent her from bumping her head on the top of the car as he put her into the back seat. She felt trapped in the confined space when he closed the door. The wire partition between the front and back seats was over a foot away but it still seemed too close to her face.

The officer got into the driver's seat and picked up his radio transmitter. "At least check out my story," she said.

"We'll do that at the station," he said. "Just relax. If you're telling the truth, you have nothing to worry about." He spoke into the radio then, a mixture of numbers and names, including a reading of his odometer and a time check, which the dispatcher verified with the station clock.

"What was that all about?" Erica asked curiously.

"Routine precaution when an unescorted male officer is transporting a female prisoner," he replied. "Makes it a little hard for a woman to claim she was raped while in custody."

"Oh," Erica said with a sigh that left her shoulders slumped. *Of course. Protect yourself, by all means. I'm only a citizen.*

The cars formed a caravan leaving the area and, once again, Erica felt as though she'd been edited into some B-grade police drama. Serial killers didn't get this kind of attention.

"You didn't read me my rights," Erica said. Surely that was a good sign.

"You're not under arrest yet," he said. "Officially. We'll take care of the formalities at the station. Unless your story checks out."

The ride to the station was under five minutes. Officer Harris parked the patrol car and radioed in his time and odometer reading again. Apparently, she wasn't considered much of a threat, because the only officer besides Harris who accompanied her inside was the tall one with the scar. It was he this time, rather than the sarcastic cop, who walked on her left as she was escorted through the drizzling rain into the building.

The ambience of the station was hardly reassuring. They couldn't have found an older, more dilapidated setting. Erica suddenly envisioned spies being tortured here during World War II, although why that image sprang to mind, she couldn't say. *Panic-laced hysteria, no doubt.*

Inside the building, she drew a lot of interest, everything from curious, evaluating perusals to ill-disguised ogles. "You working the street beat now, Harris?" asked an officer seated behind a desk.

"This is no lady of the evening," Harris said. "This is a schoolteacher."

He chortled. "You don't say. What'd she do, give some politician's kid a bad grade?"

"B and E," Harris said. "This is the perp Butler's been looking for."

That announcement threw the whole room into an unnatural silence. Erica's face flamed as she found herself the center of attention.

11

"YOU'VE GOT to be kidding!" someone said.

Apparently, the tall officer with the scar was Butler. "My sentiments exactly," he said.

"Become a cop. It's a surprise a minute," said the cop behind the desk.

"All right, guys. I've got a job to do here," Harris said. "Rash? I need your services."

A female who'd been doing paperwork at a desk stood up and walked over to them, eyeing Erica curiously.

"This is Officer Rash," Harris said. "She's going to search you again."

"I'm not armed," Erica said, trying not to sound belligerent, but no one seemed to hear.

Officer Rash was businesslike and thorough. If Erica had been packing a toothpick, it would have been found. Finishing up with an examination of Erica's socks and slippers, Officer Rash stepped back and announced, "She's clean."

Taking Erica's upper arm again, Harris led her to a metal chair facing a desk with a name plate that said Harris on it and ordered her to sit. "You'll be more comfortable here," he said, reaching behind her to unlock the cuff on her left wrist and loop it around the right arm of the chair.

Erica stretched her left arm out and rolled her shoulders. Her right arm was propped on the chair arm to which it was chained. The shackles pressured her ankles through her thick socks and the chair bottom was as hard as marble. *Oh, yes. She was comfortable now.*

Trying to be cooperative in hopes that it would facilitate the end of her nightmare, she gave him her name, birth date place of birth, and social security number; her address in Baltimore, her address in Georgia, her phone numbers; her grandmother's name, the name of the school district in which she taught. She told them she had a Georgia driver's license and plates, but she couldn't remember her license or plate numbers.

Harris took all the information, then, at a signal from Butler, he rose. "Excuse me. This won't take long."

Erica nodded. *As if she had any choice.* It wasn't as if she were going anywhere, unless she could manage to carry a chair past a whole slew of police officers.

Officers Harris and Butler conferred for what seemed like a long time, looking over at Erica from time to time. Finally, Harris returned to his desk and said, "We're going to start processing you while we check out some of this information."

"What does that mean?" Erica asked. "Processing" didn't sound good. It sounded scary. It sounded as if they were going to arrest her.

Sean. She needed him. The man, *and* the attorney. She was about to ask if she was entitled to the proverbial one phone call, when Harris answered her previous question.

"We'll take your fingerprints, get your picture—"

"Mug shots?" Erica swallowed as images of herself staring into a camera like a crazed serial killer formed in her mind. "I want to call—" *Sean* "—an attorney."

"All in good time," he said, taking the cuff from the chair arm and putting it back on her wrist. "Walk this way, please."

"This is messy, but it doesn't hurt a bit," the officer who took her fingerprints told her.

"I've done this before," she said, knowing instantly that it was the wrong thing to say when she saw the two officers exchange glances. "With my students," she explained quickly. "We had a community services officer fingerprint the entire class during our Abduction Prevention Week program."

"I've done school visitations," the fingerprinter said. "You say you're a teacher?"

Erica nodded. "Third grade."

"Well, my hat's off to you, lady," the officer said. "I'd rather face criminals one at a time than a roomful of rugrats." He stuck a paper towel in her hands. "We're done here."

It was just like a movie. Holding a sign with her name and an identification number, Erica stood in front of a ruler on the wall which showed her height to be five feet four inches. "Couldn't I at least comb my hair?" she asked. "It was windy outside and it got damp in the rain."

The cop holding the camera chuckled. "Honey, everyone we get in this studio is having a bad hair day. Just look at the camera."

The flash was harsh. Erica still had stars dancing in front of her eyes when she turned to the side as instructed. *Now what?* she wondered, although she wasn't sure she wanted to know.

The "what" that came next was being shown into a room where Officer Butler was waiting for them. Harris sat Erica at a long table, cuffing her right wrist to a metal loop, and he and Butler settled into chairs across from her.

"We want to ask you some questions, Miss O'Leary," Officer Butler said. "But first, the law dictates that we advise you of your rights."

For the first time since Harris had holstered his weapon, Erica was scared. It was a different kind of fear this time. The gun she could see and understand; being arrested was nebulous and foreign.

"Miss O'Leary, are you feeling well?" Butler asked.

She was *not* feeling well. She felt as though every drop of blood in her body had drained away. She shivered involuntarily, but she said, trying to sound strong, "I...I'm just a little cold. My shirt's damp from the rain."

Time was distorted in the spare, silent room and, although he wasn't rude or patently unfriendly, Officer Butler did little to make her comfortable. She was aware that he was watching her and, noting the mirror on the side wall, which she assumed from crime movies to be one-way glass, she wondered how many other people were watching, as well.

She listened stoically as Officer Butler advised her of her right to remain silent, warned her that anything she said could be used against her and told her she had a right to have an attorney present and that if she could not afford an attorney, one would be appointed for her.

"Yes," she answered firmly when he asked if she understood the rights he'd explained to her. Then she said, "I want to call my attorney."

"I'll take you to the phone," Harris said, unlocking the cuff.

"I . . . don't know his number," Erica said. "I have his card in my purse, but—"

"There's a bar association directory next to the phone," he said.

Her fingers were numb as she dialed the number, listened to the recording, then punched the code to get the answering service. She gave the operator her name and explained that she was at the station.

"I'll page Mr. O'Leary and give him the message. He'll contact the station."

"Oh," Erica said. "I see. Thank you." She hadn't realized how desperately she needed to hear Sean's voice until she realized she wouldn't be hearing it.

She was taken back to the interrogation room and cuffed to the table again. Officer Butler was still sitting there. "You understand that you are not required to talk to us until your attorney arrives. Do you want to wait, or do want to answer some questions?"

Erica hesitated, trying to decide what Sean would want her to do.

"The sooner you talk to us, the sooner we can get this thing resolved," Officer Butler said. "The choice is yours. We can take you to a holding cell if you want."

Erica didn't like the sound of a holding cell. So far, each place she'd been taken had been drearier than the last. "I don't mind answering questions," she said.

"Would you tell us what you were doing on the Winkle property?"

She went through the whole story again. Butler listened patiently, then said, "We have a little problem with parts of your story, Miss O'Leary. If you knew the Winkles so well—well enough to trade emergency keys—then how is it you didn't know about their alarm system?"

She explained about her grandmother, about living in Georgia, about having just returned to Baltimore. "I've only been back a few days, and I thought I'd just run into them—you know, when I was picking up the paper or something. I usually did." She sighed. "If you'd just check with the Winkles, they'll tell you—"

"We'd love to do that for you, Miss O'Leary, but the Winkles are out of the country."

"Out of the country?"

"Odd that they wouldn't mention that to you, isn't it? Or the alarm system."

Fear raised goose bumps on the back of Erica's neck. "Yes. But—I was in Georgia."

"It's also odd that you weren't listed as an authorized occupant of the property on the forms they filled out for the security company."

"I'm sure if my grandmother had been alive, they would have put her down, but with me in Georgia, maybe they just didn't think about—"

"Maybe they don't feel the same about you as they did about your grandmother," Butler said harshly.

"That's ridiculous. They certainly wouldn't be afraid I would—"

"Breaking and entering is a serious offense, Miss O'Leary. Things would go easier—"

"I wasn't breaking and entering!"

"Officer Harris responded to a call from the security company and found you trying to gain access to the house. *We* call that breaking and entering—what do you call it?"

Erica shrugged and asked meekly, "Attempt to raid a cookie jar?"

Butler scowled.

"Are you even trying to verify the information I gave you?" Erica challenged.

"We can't do much until morning," Officer Harris said. "We've been trying to get your license photo from Georgia for a positive ID, but we're having some modem problems between computers."

"A positive ID? I told you who I am."

"Until we have verification of some kind, we have no way of knowing you are who you say you are."

A knock on the door drew their attention. Harris got up, excusing himself with a nod, and disappeared into the hallway. Seconds later he returned and looked at Erica. "Your attorney is on his way."

Erica felt as though a thousand-pound yoke had been lifted from her shoulders. "Sean—Mr. O'Leary—knows me. He'll be able to verify who I am."

"Did you say O'Leary?" Harris asked.

"We're not related."

"Do you want to continue, or wait for him?"

"Let's get this over with."

She didn't like the looks that passed between the two officers. Intuition told her something was not quite right. But she had nothing to fear—did she? They would check out her story and realize she was telling the truth—wouldn't they?

Officer Butler placed a piece of paper on the table in front of him. "I've written some dates on this paper," he said. "I'd like you to look at them and see if you can remember where you were on the evenings of these dates."

He turned the list around and slid it across the table. There were perhaps a dozen entries; Erica didn't count exactly. Her mind went blank as she stared at them. Finally, she looked across the table at the cops. "This isn't just about my trying to get into the Winkles' house, is it? You think I'm involved in something else."

"There have been a number of burglaries in the area, and we have reason to believe that the perpetrator is familiar with the area."

"You think I robbed someone?" she asked incredulously.

"Robbery involves physical threat or intimidation," Harris said. "It's a harsher crime than burglary. That's why career burglars seldom carry weapons when they work. I believe you know that, Miss O'Leary. Of course, you didn't count on getting caught with a spade in your hand."

"I didn't plan on getting *caught* at all," Erica said. "I'm not a career burglar. I'm not even a recreational burglar. I'm a schoolteacher who got locked out of her house and went to the neighbor's house to get the spare key."

Officer Butler looked unconvinced. "If what you say is true, then you can help us prove it. No one can be two places at once. If you can prove you were somewhere else on these nights, you couldn't have been breaking into houses."

They were asking her for alibis! Erica sighed and looked at the list. "March eighth? I was in Georgia, of course."

"Can you remember March eighth specifically? Who you were with, where you were?"

"You can't expect a person to look at a date and immediately remember details. Maybe if I had a calendar and a date book—" She met Butler's gaze evenly. "I'm a schoolteacher in a small town. I live simply. If it was a weeknight, I was probably at home grading papers or watching television. If it was a weekend, I might have gone out with friends to a restaurant or movie. What does it matter what I was doing, anyway? I couldn't be in Georgia and Baltimore at the same time."

"You're a teacher and you live simply?"

"Yes."

"It must be difficult getting by on a teacher's salary in today's economy."

"About the same as trying to live on a cop's pay," she said pointedly.

"You have on a pretty fancy bracelet for someone living on a schoolteacher's salary."

The bracelet Sean had given her. "It was a gift," she said. "From an admirer."

"Do you have a lot of admirers who give you gifts?"

"As a matter of fact, I do," Erica said. "But most of them are under four feet tall, and most of the gifts are displayed on my refrigerator door under a magnet."

"You don't have a lot of . . . *romantic involvements?*"

"I don't see what that has to do with anything, but no."

They glared at each other across the table a moment. She saw Butler's struggle for patience before he said, in a gentle voice, "Please, Miss O'Leary. Look at the dates. See if any of them stand out."

She did as he instructed. "This one," she said. "This was the day after my grandmother's memorial service. I was here in Baltimore, staying at my grandmother's house."

"Do you remember what you did that night?"

"I think—yes. That's the night Gary and I went to the Inner Harbor and then shopped."

"Does Gary have a last name? "

"Wisdom," she said. "Mr. Wisdom. He's the vice principal at the school where I teach."

"In Georgia?"

"Yes."

"But he was here in Baltimore?"

"He's a close friend," she said. "It was spring break. He came to give me some moral support."

"Is he the dear friend who gave you the bracelet?"

"No."

"Do any of the other dates pique your memory?"

Erica skimmed them one by one until she reached the second from the bottom. "This one does," she said. "It was my birthday. I was with—"

"Gary?"

"No. I was with my attorney. He can confirm that when he gets here."

"O'Leary?"

"Yes."

"I thought he was from Baltimore."

"He is. His office is here in Towson. But he flew in—" she felt her cheeks flame as she recalled the night, the bracelet, their lovemaking "—for my birthday."

"The plot thickens," Harris said, addressing Butler.

"You can ask him when he gets here."

"Oh, we will, Miss O'Leary," Officer Butler said tiredly. "We will."

"WOULD YOU REPEAT THAT?" Sean asked. He couldn't have heard correctly. The message was the same as the first time. "Are you sure about that name?"

"I wouldn't get it wrong, Mr. O'Leary. It's almost the same as yours."

He thanked the woman distractedly and called the Towson substation. The duty officer verified that Erica was there and had been brought in after setting off an alarm while trying to burglarize a house.

If he hadn't been so concerned about Erica, he would have laughed his head off. But the thought of her in the hands of Baltimore County's finest—in any hands but his tender, loving own, actually—was enough to drive him into a near-homicidal frenzy. *What have you gotten your cute little fanny into, my dear, adorable Miss O'Leary?*

He made a quick call to his sister and then yelled for the kids. "Michael. Kaitlin. Front and center!"

They came thundering into his study from the living room, where they'd been watching a cartoon video he'd rented for them. "Get your shoes on, troops. You're going to Aunt Kathy's."

"We just got home from Aunt Kathy's," Kaitlin said.

"We have movies," Michael said.

Sean's shoulders drooped. "I know, guys. But Daddy has an emergency. You can take your movies with you. Your cousins will enjoy them, too."

"They won't want to watch *Cinderella*," Kaitlin said.

Sean pulled her into his arms for a hug. "Poor Kaitlin. It's not easy being the youngest *and* the only girl, is it?"

His daughter nodded solemnly, and Sean said, "I'll make sure you get to see *Cinderella*, even if we have to keep the movie an extra day. Now, you two go pack your pj's and clothes for the morning in case you have to spend the night."

"Daddy," Kaitlin protested with a pathetic puppy-dog look.

"Move it!" Sean ordered. *I feel guilty enough already. I'm only one person.*

He would have referred anyone else in the world to a criminal attorney and stayed home, but this was Erica. Surely a man was entitled to some romantic involvements—even single fathers.

"You're going to owe me big time," his sister said once Michael and Kaitlin had disappeared into her house.

Yet again, he was feeling guilty. And apologizing. "I swear, I'll enroll them in day care if Mrs. Smead isn't back by the end of the week."

"It won't be the end of the world, you know," Kathy said. "Lots of kids go to day care."

"Most of them have mothers who pick them up at the end of the day."

"And a lot of them don't have fathers to tuck them in at night. Quit beating yourself up, Sean. You do the best you can. That's all any parent can do—especially a single parent."

Sean nodded roughly. "Well, this single parent has to get to the police station."

"You know what you need, don't you?" his sister asked.

Sean frowned. "We've had this conversation before, but you might as well say it. No visit is complete until you do."

"You need a woman."

Sean grinned diabolically. "Maybe I'll find one at the police station."

Her eyes narrowed suspiciously. "I heard you were seeing someone by the name of O'Leary. From down south somewhere—Georgia, I believe? Isn't that where you went flying off to last month to see a client about a dog? Oh, no. It must have been a *cat.*"

She cackled aloud at his reaction. "Don't bother dissembling. I can tell from your face I'm onto something."

"I have to get to the police station" Sean growled.

She grinned. "Cardinal rule of parenting number 106— *never* expect your children to keep your secrets."

"You're as big a pain in the butt now as you were growing up," Sean said over his shoulder as he walked toward his car.

"You shouldn't harass a sister you're relying on to baby-sit," Kathy called after him. She had never been one to let him get in the last word.

A short drive brought him to the Towson substation. He presented his identification and demanded to see Erica.

"The schoolteacher?" the sergeant asked. "She's in the interrogation room. I'll find somebody to take you back."

"Make it quick," Sean said. *The interrogation room! They probably had a bare light bulb shining in her face.*

And she was probably scared to death.

He gritted his teeth as he was shown to the door and the officer with him knocked. *If they had hurt one hair on her head—*

Erica was at the table. Dwarfed by the disproportionate size of the heavy table in the closetlike room, she looked more like one of her students than the competent teacher he knew her to be. Her hair was mussed, and her hand, fingertips stained black with ink, looked small enough to slip through the cuff manacling it to a metal loop on the table top.

The moment she recognized him, her face lit up with relief and, crying his name, she rose to run to him. Or tried to. The wrist cuff stopped her progress short, just as two officers, both of them above average in size, lunged to intercept her.

"Sit down!" a rough-looking cop barked at Erica. He turned his attention to Sean. "Advise your client, Counselor."

"Get me out of here!" Erica pleaded with an edge of hysteria.

Sean looked at Erica and smiled reassuringly. "Hang in there." He glowered at the cop. "I'd like to talk privately with my client."

The cop nodded. "You'll get your chance. But first—"

"No 'But firsts,'" Sean said. "I want to talk to her *now*."

The cop cocked his head and spoke in a man-to-man confidential tone. "Simmer down, Counselor. I think it would be in your client's best interest for you to listen to what I have to tell you before the two of you confer. Have a seat. And you—" he pointed his finger at Erica "—sit still and don't . . . say . . . a word."

"You don't have to talk to her that way," Sean said. Turning to Erica, he added, "Don't say a thing."

"Mr. O'Leary?" The officer bobbed his head toward an empty chair.

"This had better be good," Sean grumbled, dropping into the chair.

"We've got a bit of a situation here. Your client is a suspect in a series of burglaries. We asked her to look at a list of dates to see if she could establish an alibi, and guess who she says she was with one of the nights in question."

Sean's eyebrows shot up.

"Bingo!" Butler said. He pressed his forefinger on the list of dates and pushed it to Sean. "Do any of these dates ring a bell?" He cast a warning look in Erica's direction. "And no coaching, please."

Sean could almost hear the frustrated rage Erica was biting back. All things considered, she appeared to be holding up well, but she was tottering, and it wouldn't take much to send her over the edge. He focused his attention on the list of dates, then grinned at Erica. "May sixteenth is Miss O'Leary's birthday. I flew to Georgia and we had dinner."

"Well, it's consistent, anyway," Butler said heavily. "I don't suppose you have any solid evidence to back this up?"

"I charged my airfare," he said. "I might even—" He put his briefcase on the table and opened it. "I just happen to have my ticket. I remember seeing it the last time I went rummaging through here." He handed the folder to the cop. "My name, the date, round trip Baltimore to Savannah. The rental-car receipt is probably in there, too. The mileage should figure just about the round-trip distance between the Savannah airport and Miss O'Leary's apartment."

"You don't mind if I hold on to these items for verification?" Butler asked.

Sean smiled cunningly. "Not if you give me an itemized receipt and photocopies of them."

Butler threw his hands in the air in a gesture of frustration. "I'll run the copies while you confer with your client."

Sean said, "Could I have a word with you and Officer Harris first?"

Butler shrugged. "Whatever you say, Counselor. Harris, get Rash in here. Miss O'Leary would probably appreciate a comfort break by now."

Sean leaned over and whispered into Erica's ear, "Trust me."

She nodded tersely, saying nothing, but the look in her eyes a few minutes later as the female officer led her out of the room was enough to make a man look for a dragon to slay for her.

Sean had to settle for Officers Butler and Harris. "All right, gentlemen," he said, looking from one cop to the other. "We're all professionals here. First I want to know what you've got—or think you've got. And then we can work out what it's going to take to get Miss O'Leary out of here."

12

ACCORDING TO the station clock, Erica had been cuffed to the chair in front of Officer Harris's desk for twenty-two minutes. To Erica, it seemed more like twenty-two days. *What was taking Sean so long?*

Was she in deeper trouble than she'd thought?

Sean, where are you? Why are you keeping me in suspense like this? You were anxious to talk to me when you first got here—what happened to change that?

Harris emerged from the interrogation room and accepted a stack of papers from the officer at the main desk. He glanced at Erica over the tops of the paper from time to time as he read.

Another five, then ten minutes crawled by before, finally, Sean and the other officer came into the room. "I'm out of here," Officer Butler told the sergeant on his way out of the building.

Erica took heart from the pleased expression on Sean's face as he and Butler walked toward the desk. Harris, key in hand, knelt to unlock the shackles.

"You're releasing me?" Erica asked, afraid to believe it.

"I'm releasing you into Mr. O'Leary's custody until three o'clock tomorrow afternoon," Harris said as the leg irons fell away from Erica's ankles.

But when he moved to release the cuff attaching her wrist to the chair arm, Sean's half smile turned into a cocky grin. "Hold off on that a minute," he told the cop.

Erica and Harris both looked at him as though he'd lost his mind. Still grinning, Sean leaned to whisper in her ear, "Say it."

She gave him a blank look.

"Say it," he whispered again.

"You're enjoying this," she accused.

Sean's grin grew. "Say you were glad to see me, and the nice policeman will unlock the cuff."

"Oh, all right!" she snapped. "I was glad to see you!"

He curved his hand behind his ear and tilted his head toward her. "A little louder, please."

"I was glad to see you." She pushed the words through gritted teeth.

Gloating, Sean nodded to Harris, and the large cop removed the cuffs from her wrists. Erica stood up. Sean's eyes filled with warmth as their gazes met. "Now you can show me," he said softly.

His name tore from her throat as she wrapped her arms around his waist and buried her face in his chest.

"I knew I should have been an attorney," a cop wisecracked.

Sean and Erica exchanged sheepish grins. Sean gently whispered into her ear, "Let's get out of here before they change their minds."

"I thought you'd never ask."

With his left arm tucked around Erica, Sean extended his right hand to Officer Harris. "We'll see you at three o'clock tomorrow."

Harris cast a tough-cop scowl at Sean. "Don't make me sorry for being easy, O'Leary."

"We'll be here," Sean assured him.

The rain had stopped, leaving a mist rising from the pavement and puddles in the streets. It could have been pouring and Erica would have thought it was glorious. She stopped, threw her head back against Sean's shoulder and sucked in fresh, cool air. "It wasn't because you're an attorney," she said, savoring having his strength to lean on. "It was because you're . . . you."

He tightened his arm around her. "If you're as smart as I think you are, you'll be damned glad I'm also a fine attorney—especially since criminal law isn't my specialty. If I hadn't done some fancy dancing in there, you'd be on your way to the women's detention center for the night."

They walked to his car. "They were really going to put me in jail, weren't they?" Erica said as Sean drove out of the parking lot.

"Pending arraignment in the morning," he said. "I convinced them to hold off until they finished checking out the information you gave them."

"I can't believe I got *arrested!*"

"Technically, you were taken into custody. You weren't officially arrested."

"Well, it felt official when Harris stuck his gun in my face."

"In your face?"

"At my chest, okay?" Erica said sharply. "It was just as scary."

Sean covered her hand with his. "I know it was."

Erica didn't want to cry, but it was everything she could do to rein in the threatening tears. She brought her fist crashing down on the dashboard. "It's so *stupid!* If they would just ask the Winkles—"

"Do you know Mrs. Winkle's sister?"

"Edith?"

"Good. Does she know you—or more to the point, is she aware that the Winkles keep a key to your house?"

"Of course she is. She used to get the key to the Winkles' house from my grandmother when she dropped by and the Winkles weren't at home."

"If she tells Butler what you've just told me, you'll be in good shape."

"Is Butler Harris's superior or something?"

"He has more seniority. But that's not why he's on this case like a bear on a beehive. Butler's nursing a personal vendetta for this cat burglar who's working Towson. It's driving him crazy. When Harris caught you red-handed, they were both convinced they'd found their man—or woman, as the case may be."

"Lucky me," Erica said.

"Put yourself in their place, Erica. You had no ID, you set off that alarm and you're dressed like a cat burglar. Butler was salivating."

"How did you talk them into letting me go?"

"Their case was falling apart with every piece of new information. I was able to confirm your identification and place you in Georgia on the night of one of the burglaries. They finally got your driver's license on-line from Georgia Highway, and the photos and signatures matched. Your prints didn't even come close to matching the prints they'd lifted at two of the scenes. Of course, they want someone at County to look them over before they rule out a match completely. And they'll verify your employment when the school district offices open in the morning."

"Everyone in Georgia is going to hear about this," Erica lamented aloud.

"Not *everyone*," Sean said drolly. "You're small potatoes compared to the Olympics. Besides not everyone in Atlanta watches the evening news."

"Everyone I care about will hear it," she said. "And most folks figure that where there's smoke, there's fire somewhere."

"Anyone who believes that you're capable of burglary isn't a friend and never will be."

"I could lose my job over this."

"They have no grounds to fire you unless you're convicted of something."

"They'll find a way if they decide to do it—or they'll just make me so miserable I'll finally quit."

"Don't expect sympathy from me on this subject," Sean said. "I want you here in Baltimore, not way down 'pon the Suwannee River."

"That's easy for you to say."

"It's not as easy as you seem to think," Sean said, turning his head to look at her. "I know what I'm asking implies."

Erica reminded herself that eight hours ago she couldn't get him on the phone. They had a lot to sort out between them before she'd think about changing her entire life to accommodate his.

"If I leave Suwannee Elementary, I want it to be my idea," she said. "I don't want a termination on my record." Suddenly realizing that they were riding in the opposite direction from her house, she asked, "Where are we going?"

"To my place," Sean said. "That was part of the deal with Butler. He was concerned that you might start unloading evidence before he has a chance to get a warrant for your house and car, so I had to agree to take you straight to my house and bring you directly to the station tomorrow."

"Can he do that—get a warrant to search my house?"

"If Mrs. Winkle's sister doesn't verify that you have the Winkles' permission to enter their house when they're not at home, he's got a good shot at a warrant. But he agreed to hold off going to the judge until he talks to her."

Erica crossed her arms and shifted restlessly in the passenger seat. "I'd just have to break in if I went home now anyway." She sighed. "What am I going to do about clothes?"

"I'll find something for you to sleep in."

Sleep. The implications of going to his house for the night suddenly became clear to her. "Sean, I called you tonight in a professional capacity. Just because—"

"I wasn't making any assumptions about sleeping arrangements, Erica. I just thought you'd be more comfortable at my house than at the women's detention center."

Erica buried her face in her hands and sighed again. "I will. I . . . oh, Sean—"

He patted her shoulder. "Hang in there. Just a few more blocks." He turned onto a driveway that led to the detached garage behind a sprawling single-story home. In the backyard, a tire swing hung from the limb of an oak tree, and a ladder led up to a log playhouse designed like a fort.

"Will your children still be awake?" Erica asked as they walked to the house.

"They're at my sister's," he said. "She lives down the street and around the corner."

The back door opened into a laundry room which looked as though it might explode if someone didn't start washing the baskets of dirty laundry soon. "Excuse the mess," he said. "My housekeeper is still in New Jersey."

"Did it ever occur to you that you might be able to operate this complex piece of machinery on your own?" she asked, putting her hand on the washing machine.

"I was planning to do that tonight," he said, "but one of my clients got herself picked up on a breaking and entering charge and I had to go negotiate her fanny out of jail."

"I'm sorry," she said. "I'm . . . so—" Suddenly, everything came crashing down around her. She couldn't hold on to her composure any longer. Nor could she resist the comfort of Sean's arms around her or deny herself the comfort of his strength.

"You have nothing to apologize for," he said, holding her. "You didn't plan—"

"I just went out to the car to get the books and m-movies," she said, choking back a sob.

His hands stroked her back soothingly. "You didn't do anything wrong. It was all a horrible misunderstanding."

"He pointed a g-gun at me." She burrowed her cheek into the front of his shirt.

He kissed her temple. "Go ahead. Let it out."

"They put me in chains," she said, sniffing. "Like a criminal." A woeful sob tore from her throat. "I just wanted to have a quiet evening, and now my moo goo gai pan is sitting on the table spoiling and the movies and books probably got soaked in the rain."

"You didn't get dinner?" She shook her head against his chest. He kissed her temple again. "We'll figure something out. In the meantime, I know exactly what you need." Stepping back, he opened the clothes dryer and brought out a thick terry bath towel and stuffed it into her arms. "Follow me."

The laundry room led to the breakfast nook, the breakfast nook to the family room, the family room to a long hallway. He stopped outside a bathroom festooned with bathtub toys and children's sparkle toothpaste. Gesturing for her to wait, he stepped into the room and pondered several cartoon-figure plastic bottles on the rim of the tub, musing aloud, "Mighty Morphin Power Ranger, Scooby-Doo…ah, here we go. Little Mermaid."

Grinning, he reentered the hall. "Come on. I'm going to make a mermaid out of a suspected cat burglar."

The master suite was at the end of the hall, tastefully furnished in contemporary furniture of blond wood. The king-size bed was rumpled on one side, the pillow misshapened by the imprint of Sean's head, the cranberry-colored quilted bedspread folded back to reveal white sheets with cranberry pinstripes. Erica would have bet a hundred-dollar bill that his housekeeper had bought those sheets.

Or his wife. The thought disturbed her. She didn't even know how long his wife had been dead. When it came down to it, she had to admit that she knew very little about him. Here, in this house with a tree swing in the backyard and dirty clothes in the laundry room, he was totally different from the cocky Irish attorney who'd tried to pick her up in the lounge car on the train.

But not from the man who'd shared that sleeper with her. Who'd held her while she cried. Who'd flown to Georgia to wish her happy birthday.

The suggestion of a smile, bittersweet and tentative, touched her lips as she followed him into the bathroom. *He'd brought her a gold bracelet with a train on it—did he know he'd left Georgia with her heart?*

"It's all yours," Sean said, gesturing toward a shell-shaped sunken tub. The faux marble was off-white with a subtle hint of rose shading, veined by the same cranberry as the bedspread in the adjacent room. Handing her the bubble bath, he took the towel and draped it over the bar then bent over, closed the drain on the tub and turned on the taps. "Soak this whole horrible episode out of your system," he ordered. "I'm going to rustle up something for you to eat. Yell if you need anything."

A few minutes later, Erica sank into a sea of warm water and a cloudlike foam of bubbles, immediately feeling the talons of tension release their hold on her. She slipped down until her neck rested against the rounded headrest built into the rim of the tub and closed her eyes. *How had he known?* she wondered. *How had he known* exactly *what she needed?*

She opened her eyes and looked around the room, noting the cranberry bath mat, the rose-beige wallpaper with tiny cranberry flowers on delicate green stems, the vanity with twin sinks. One of the sinks was surrounded by Sean's things—a razor, hair dryer, styling brush, toothbrush, toothpaste. The other sink was surrounded by . . . nothing. Nothing female. Nothing even human. No facial cleansers or makeup or hair sprays. No combs or brushes or eyelash curlers. No bottles of perfume or lotion or after-bath splashes to dilute the scent of Sean's after-shave, which permeated the bathroom like a benign ghost.

His wife had been dead a long time—long enough for the traces of her everyday life to have been cleared away. *By whom?* she wondered. Sean, desperately trying to deal with his grief? A supportive female friend or relative? The housekeeper?

Relieved that his wife's presence no longer haunted the bathroom they'd shared, she nevertheless found that unused, unadorned sink sad. The thought of a man like Sean living alone, raising children alone, was sad. The thought of his children without a mother was sad.

Erica closed her eyes again and took a deep breath. *Oh, Sean. You manipulated the truth, but I was blind. I didn't see—*

There was a knock at the door. "Erica? Are you covered with bubbles?"

Erica looked at the mountain of bubbles capping the water like meringue on a pie and smiled. "Yes."

"I brought you some dinner." Carrying a tray, he gingerly entered the room. "This is all I could find. I'm going to have to break down and go to the grocery store soon, but for now, this ought to stave off starvation."

He put the tray down next to the tub within her reach. The metal tray was decorated with a portrait of Kermit the Frog dressed as a pirate. On it were a bowl of macaroni and cheese—the creamy, shell kind from a box—a bowl of strawberries, a red rose from the climbing bush she'd noticed near the back door and two glasses of wine.

"The strawberries are fresh," he said. "They're from my sister's patch." She was staring at the tray. Sean waited for her reaction. Having nothing to offer a woman but macaroni and cheese was embarrassing, especially when the woman had been through what Erica had just endured. "You don't have to eat it if you don't—" His breath caught in his throat. There was a tear on her cheek. "Erica?"

Slowly, she tilted her head to look at his face. Her eyes were overbright, filled with tears. "It's the most romantic meal anyone has ever made for me."

Exhaling, Sean sank to the rim of the tub and stared adoringly at her face. "Does this mean I'm forgiven?"

"For serving me macaroni and cheese?"

"For... everything," he said. "Erica—"

"You're too far away," she said. "I want you near me."

Sean smiled. "Do I get in, or do you want to get out?"

She responded with a smile of invitation as she slid deeper into the water. "I'm too comfortable to get out yet."

He reached for the buckle of his belt. "Then I'll just have to get in."

Erica watched him undress, admiring his broad chest, long legs and firm buttocks. A myriad of sensations blended as he settled beside her: the warmth of the water and the heat of the man; the silky slickness of the soap and the gentle, grating roughness of the hair on his legs; the sensual pleasure of having the water slide caressingly over her skin and the sexual pleasure of his body touching hers; the indulgence of idling in the tub for the sole purpose of relaxation; the idea that they were together in such an intimate way, touching, becoming aroused, knowing where it would lead but taking their time.

Sean picked up the bowl of macaroni and the spoon. "Close your eyes and open your mouth," he instructed. He fed her a spoonful of the creamy entrée. "This may taste like macaroni and cheese, but it's actually moo goo gai pan."

Erica almost choked on the cheesy pasta as she giggled and swallowed at the same time. "I'm sorry. It's just . . . it's a long stretch from cheese to Chinese vegetables." Sean frowned, and she said quickly, "It's all right, Sean. I *like* macaroni and cheese."

Spoonful by spoonful, he fed her the rest of the pasta, reducing Erica to helpless laughter by playfully making airplane noises or buzzing like a bee while moving the spoon in circles in the air between the bowl and her mouth. Finally, when the bowl was almost empty, Erica told him, "That's enough. I'm full."

Sean put the bowl back on the tray, picked up the wineglasses and gave her one. They sipped in silence a moment before Erica suddenly burst out laughing again.

"The wine couldn't have acted that quickly," Sean observed with a grin.

Erica took a deep breath to control the laughter. "What did you do on your summer vacation, Miss O'Leary?" she asked in a childlike falsetto. Then, in her normal voice, she answered, "I got arrested breaking into the neighbor's house and then my attorney took me home with him and fed me macaroni and cheese in the bathtub when we were both naked."

She'd never been more beautiful to him. Her face was flushed from the steamy water, her eyes bright—with amusement now instead of tears—her hair still riotously mussed, her features relaxed.

"It's good to see you laughing," he said.

Her smile faded to a pleasant expression. "You haven't known me during my happiest moments, have you?"

"Your birthday was pretty special."

"It was more special because of you, and—" The color in her cheeks deepened, telling him she was thinking of their lovemaking. Quickly, she took a sip of wine.

Sean sipped his wine, too. "Erica—"

After a beat of silence, she said, "We have to talk about it."

Sean nodded. He'd been about to say the same thing. They couldn't reminisce about the pleasure they'd shared without ultimately arriving at the unresolved disagreement they'd had. But where should they begin?

At the source, of course. And the source of their disagreement had been his failure to tell her about Janet. Steeling himself, he said, "My wife was killed in an automobile accident three years ago."

"Oh, Sean. I'm sorry."

Of all the people who'd said those same words since Janet's death, she had the least motivation to mean them, but he could feel her sincerity.

"Janet and I started dating in high school," he went on. "I was always a little shy around girls, but it was different with Janet. We'd actually known each other since grade school. I could talk to her without getting tongue-tied or turning purple."

"I can't imagine you tongue-tied."

"I'm not sixteen anymore." He rested his neck against the headrest next to Erica's. "Trust me—at sixteen I was tongue-tied every time I got within five feet of an attractive female."

"Except for Janet," Erica said, grinning.

"Janet wasn't a female. She was . . . Janet. Until one day— she walked past us in her gym clothes, and one of my friends made a comment about . . . certain parts of her anatomy. Suddenly I saw her in a whole new way." He laughed softly. "I'd never noticed before. The next time I talked to her, my palms were sweaty and I couldn't string two words together. But she was as nice as always, and I persevered." He sighed. "I wouldn't tell you all this if it . . . if you weren't—" He shrugged. "It seems I still get a little tongue-tied around females I'm trying to impress."

"You don't have to be afraid of me," she said, sliding her hand up his shin to his knee. Although arousing, the movement was more intimate than sexual.

Sean put his left hand over hers where it rested on his knee and looked at her face. "I'm in unchartered waters here, if you'll forgive the pun," he said. "Erica, there weren't any girls before Janet, and there haven't been any women since—except you."

He watched the shock capture her face, then set his wineglass on the tray and touched her cheek with his fingertips. "You see now why I was nervous that first time in your apartment."

"You aren't sorry, are you?" she asked.

"That we made love? God, Erica. No." *How could she possibly think that?* "I just don't have a lot of experience dealing with this sort of thing. I was hoping it would happen, but I didn't want to rush things. I hadn't planned on it happening that night. I didn't want you to think that seducing you was my only reason for going to Georgia."

"*Why* did you come to Georgia?"

"Because— Damn it, Erica—isn't it obvious? I wanted to see you." His hand slid from her face, over her neck to cap her shoulder. *Her mouth was so close to his.* "If I made a mistake by not telling you about Janet, it was an error in judgment, not a deliberate deception. Three years seems like a long time—an eternity—but I'm still handling everything one new situation at a time. And you definitely fall under the heading of a new situation."

"I'm really the only woman you've been with since your wife died?" Her eyes were as full of wonder as a child's at the circus.

"I hope that tells you something about the kind of man I am and the way I feel about you," Sean said.

The next thing he knew, she was sprawled on top of him, cradling his face in her hands and kissing him hungrily, her slick wet breasts pressed against his chest, her stomach soft, her thighs velvety. Under her weight, his buttocks lost traction on the slippery bottom of the tub and he slipped down, inadvertently pulling her with him, until their faces were almost submerged. He braced his palms against the bottom and pushed himself into a sitting position. Parting her legs, Erica settled astride him, facing him, her bottom fitting cozily atop his thighs. Sean covered her breasts, kneading with his fingers until the peaks hardened against his palms, and as he watched her eyes glaze with passion, he desired her with a terrifying intensity.

"I . . . didn't . . . bring anything," she said breathlessly, her voice hoarse with arousal.

"I have what we need," he said, lowering his hands to mold her ribs, then around her waist and down to cradle her bottom, pulling her closer until they were as close as they could be without an actual joining. Her sultry sighs seeped into his senses.

Guiding her gently aside, he rose and reached for the towel. Fully aroused, he experienced a moment of embarrassment, but he forgot his self-consciousness when he took her hand to help her up and caught sight of her glistening body. Soapy water flowed in rivulets over her curves, and cloudlike puffs of suds clung to her skin in small patches. She was beautiful, a wraith, a temptress.

Sean wrapped the towel around her, patting her dry. Capturing his gaze with her own, Erica draped her arms across his shoulders and twined her hands behind his neck, urging his head down until their mouths met in an urgent mating.

They made their way into the bedroom and fell onto the mattress together. Their lovemaking this time was different from the sweet, tentative exploration at her apartment, or the cozy, familiar coupling on her grandmother's sofa. They were desperate for each other. Bodies linked, they rolled and thrust mindlessly, twisting the bedding into a chaotic lump as they sought and, ultimately, found physical release in each other's arms.

"Did that really happen?" Erica said afterward as they lay together, their limbs as tangled as the sheets.

"If it *didn't*, it was one incredible fantasy," Sean said.

"I thought sex like that only happened on prime-time soap operas."

"They couldn't put what we just did on film," Sean said. "The camera would melt."

Her sigh of contentment ruffled the hair on his chest. "I wish I could see if you were smiling," he said.

"I am," she said. "Every...single...inch of me is smiling."

"I'm not sure there's an inch of me that's ever going to be *able* to move again."

She kissed his cheek. "How about a bath?"

"We just got out of the tub."

"The water's probably still warm," Erica said, extricating herself from his arms. "Come on, it'll relax you."

"If I get any more relaxed, the next phase will be *rigor mortis*."

"Suit yourself," Erica taunted, getting out of bed. "*I'm* going to get back in that wonderful tub."

Sean grinned as he watched her sashay into the bathroom in that strictly female way she had of moving. *Maybe he could move, at least as far as the bathroom. By way of the kitchen, where he could get the bottle of wine he'd opened earlier—*

Carrying the bottle, he entered the bathroom. The bubbles had dissipated except for a few scattered patches, and he could make out the silhouette of her legs stretched out in front of her. Her arms were spread along the rim of the tub and her breasts, partially submerged, were fully exposed.

She smiled as he approached. "I thought you were too tired to move."

"I thought you might be thirsty," he said, lifting the bottle. A dumb, schoolboy grin slid onto his face. "I missed you."

His right leg aligned with her left as he got into the tub on the opposite side from her, facing her. Erica, nearest the tray, handed him the glasses one by one to fill. He filled them, put the bottle down and raised his glass. "To...*sex!*"

"Great sex," Erica said, touching her goblet to his and laughing sensually.

They drank the wine in mellow silence. When her glass was empty, Erica set it on the tray and picked up the rose and smelled it. "I don't get it, Sean," she said abruptly. "You obviously enjoy sex."

"What was your first clue?" Sean asked wryly.

"You must have met dozens of women who would have been willing. Why—"

She left the question unspoken, but Sean knew what it was. He shook his head. "After Janet and the baby were killed—

"You lost a baby, too?"

Sean frowned. It still hurt to remember. "Janet was five months pregnant with our third child," he said. "They took the baby by caesarean at the hospital, but she was just too premature, and they were too late. Janet had been killed instantly, and by the time they got to the hospital—" He exhaled wearily. "She didn't suffer. That was the only comfort."

"You must have been—" Again, she didn't need to complete the thought for Sean to grasp her meaning.

"She . . . *we* . . . wanted a houseful of kids. She'd always wanted at least four, and she'd had to wait so long to start a family. Until I got out of law school. Then she had Michael and Kaitlin. We were so happy and . . . *normal*. It just never occurred to me that she might be driving home from the grocery store and get killed."

He put his wineglass on the tray. "It was so senseless. There was no one to blame. If she'd been hit by a drunk driver, at least I would have been able to express some rage. I could have blamed someone."

He paused, looking at Erica's face, feeding on the understanding in her eyes. "But it wasn't a yuppie who'd had one too many cocktails, it was a kid. A teenager who'd had his driver's license two days. Not a bad kid, just a boy feeling his oats and doing seventy in a forty-mile zone who hit a slick spot in the road and skidded into the wrong lane."

Erica spread her hand over his knee, quietly comforting him. Sean released a dismal sigh. "He died, too. I saw his parents at the hospital—" He paused, swallowing. "My sister says I'm overprotective with the kids. I think that's why—I can't help wondering how I'll be able to let them get behind the wheel of a car. It's hard to let them do anything, to let go."

"It's hard for any parent to let go," Erica said, her voice soft and sympathetic.

"After it happened, I couldn't think about any other woman," he went on. "Not in a romantic context. But after a while, I came out of the fog far enough to notice that women were interested in me. Some of them were willing to use my kids to get to me. When I finally wised up to what was going on, I vowed to make sure it never happened again."

"That's why you didn't tell me about the children."

"I don't share that part of my life with anyone," he said. "I don't want anyone using my kids to get to me, and I don't want a string of women going in and out of my children's lives. They're well cared for, but they have no mother, and that makes them vulnerable. I don't want them confused."

Erica's eyes were bright. "You let *me* meet your children."

"Am I scaring you?"

"A little."

"Good. Because I'm terrified of losing you. I don't want you to go back to Georgia."

She chewed on her bottom lip as she contemplated how to respond. "I don't have to make that decision for a while yet. Maybe we should just work on getting to know each other better and see how we both feel in August."

Sean nodded. After a prolonged silence, he said, "I've told you a lot about myself tonight. Tell me something about you."

Erica thought a moment and then grinned mischievously. "I have very talented feet."

Sean chortled. "What can your feet do?"

"Watch, and be wowed," Erica said smugly. Then, with her toes, she plucked a strawberry from the bowl on the tray and pressed it against Sean's mouth.

Sean playfully bit her toes along with the strawberry and she yanked her foot away. He swallowed the strawberry and said, "I'm afraid to ask what else you can do."

Erica lowered her leg into the water between his. "Bet I can think of a creative way to play footsie."

"Yes," Sean agreed as she wiggled her talented toes. "Oh, yes."

13

ERICA AWOKE at nine the next morning to find a cat's face an inch above hers. "Esmerelda," she said. "Hello. I'd forgotten you were here." The cat meowed indignantly, and Erica scratched her behind the ears. "Where's Sean? What'd you do with him?"

The cat's purr told her nothing, but a note on Sean's pillow answered her questions. He'd gone to his office but would be back by noon with lunch. He'd left a T-shirt on the bed for her to wear around the house.

Deciding she might as well make herself useful, she went through the dirty-clothes baskets and sorted out a load of the children's shorts, shirts and socks and threw them in the washer before settling down with the morning paper, a glass of juice and Esmerelda.

She skimmed the headlines and comics and then, unable to resist the opportunity to find out more about the people who lived here, she walked through the house. The children's rooms were readily identifiable. Michael's was papered in bright blue-and-white stripes and low shelving held model rockets, cars, Mighty Morphin Power Rangers and several buckets of interlocking plastic building blocks. Buzz Lightyear grinned down from a poster on the wall, and a growth chart with a life-size likeness of a popular basketball player covered the door.

Kaitlin's room was done in narrow pastel ribbon stripes. A blackboard-easel stood in one corner next to a worktable cluttered with paper and crayons. Stacking storage cubes held a menagerie of stuffed animals, and cartoon-character cut-outs of cute, cuddly animals from popular children's films adorned the wall.

The living room was decorated in conservative earth tones. The focal point of the room, as far as Erica was concerned, was a framed portrait on the mantel of the brick fireplace. Captured in soft focus with perfect lighting, it was the picture of a young woman in a long, pastel dress seated in a rocking chair cradling an infant in a lace-edged christening gown in her arms. A toddler boy, Michael in miniature, dressed in a sailor-suit coverall with short pants, stood next to the chair, cautiously touching the baby's head as he stared at its tiny face in awe.

Janet O'Leary. Erica studied the picture for a long time, searching the face of Sean's wife. She could see traces of Kaitlin in the softness of the features and the fair hair. Janet O'Leary had been pretty, but the overwhelming impression she gave was of gentleness. Her affection for her children glowed in her Mona Lisa smile and the love the camera had captured in her eyes. Her hand rested lightly on the skirt of the christening gown, the diamond solitaire and wedding band on her ring finger both elegant and tasteful.

What do she and I have in common that drew Sean O'Leary's attention? Erica asked silently. *Are we alike somehow?* She forced herself to turn away. She wasn't going to play that game. If Sean hadn't been ready to let go, he wouldn't have shown up in Georgia on her birthday.

Hearing the washer cycle finish, she went to the laundry room to put the wet clean clothes into the dryer and start a second load of kid-size washing. By the time Sean returned, she was fully dressed in her jeans and Sean's shirt, her hair was brushed and pulled into a neat ponytail and she was folding the second load of laundry while load three dried and load four washed.

"What's this?" Sean said, spying the stacks of folded shirts. "You didn't have to do that."

She shrugged. "Just trying to help out." She added a folded shirt to Michael's stack and rose to greet Sean. "But I want it on record that I am not establishing a precedent. I'm just doing you a favor under special circumstances."

"Noted," he said. "And I want it on record that I appreciate it."

She gave him a quick kiss, then eyed the white paper bag he was carrying. "What's for lunch?"

"Moo goo gai pan, and shrimp fried rice."

Erica flashed him a coquettish smile. "You may just get a *big* kiss!"

They tried to eat with chopsticks, critiquing each other's style and laughing at their general ineptitude before resorting to forks to finish the meal.

After they'd cleared away the paper cartons and other lunch debris, Sean retired to his desk in the corner of the family room to go over some paperwork he'd brought from his office. Erica finished the last few loads of laundry and then stretched out on the worn sofa a few feet away to read magazines until it was time to leave for the police station.

"Nervous?" Sean asked once they were in the car, although her pallor and subdued silence made the question pointless.

"What do you think?" she asked. "I may be on my way to the big house."

Sean knew he shouldn't laugh, but he couldn't help it. "You are *not* headed to the big house," he assured her. "At the very worst, you'll be arrested and arraigned. In that case, I'll bail you out and take you back to my place while they search your house."

"Thanks for that reassuring pep talk," Erica said. "I feel much better now."

"Whatever happens, try to look calm and concerned, but not worried."

"That's easy for you to say."

"I'm an attorney. We have ice water in our veins."

She crossed her arms over her waist and exhaled heartily. "You didn't feel cold last night."

Sean grinned. "It was the hot bathwater."

"I'd feel a lot more confident if I were wearing real shoes. If I end up in front of a judge, I'm going to feel ridiculous in my house slippers."

"Let's just hope it doesn't come to that."

It didn't. Butler was waiting for them. Erica felt reassured immediately when he didn't handcuff her to the chair as he gestured for them to sit down in front of his desk.

"Your story checks out," Butler said without preamble. "The school district verified your employment and your principal confirmed that you had an excellent attendance record. Mrs. Winkle's sister assured me that her sister indeed keeps a key to Marian Stonehouse's home—your home now—in the cookie jar on the counter. She also said that her sister had asked her to keep an eye out for you when she went to the Winkles' house to feed their fish so she could warn you that the Winkles had installed a security system. They had been nervous about leaving their house unoccupied for three weeks because of the recent string of burglaries in the area."

He opened his top desk drawer and took out a brown envelope with his name written on it. Lifting the flap, he shook the contents onto the desktop. Erica recognized the key she'd given her neighbor by the bright yellow yarn Mrs. Winkle had threaded through the eye of it. "She dropped this by this morning and asked me to give it to you and convey her apologies."

"May I?" Erica asked, reaching for the key.

"By all means," Officer Butler said. "Take it and get out of here. Just try not to go setting off any more alarm systems."

"Next time I go outside, my keys go with me, if I have to wear them around my neck," Erica assured him.

Sean rose and shook the cop's hand. "Thank you for your fairness, Officer Butler."

"Just doing my duty, Counselor," Butler replied. "Contrary to popular belief, we're here to protect citizens, not harass them. Now, if you don't mind, I have a real criminal to track down."

Erica accosted Sean the moment they were through the door of the station, hugging him and dropping kisses all over his face. "Thank you. Thank you. Thank you."

Sean tried to be stern and stoic, but a grin tugged at the corners of his mouth as he said, "Miss O'Leary. Please. Try to restrain yourself. We're in public."

She looped her arm around his. "I don't care who sees how grateful I am, but for the sake of your professional image—"

"You might not be so grateful when you find out what my fee is."

Erica shrugged away his concern. "Whatever it is, it was worth it. And as you well know, I can afford a good lawyer."

"I wasn't planning on billing you," he said. "I want to work it out in trade."

Erica's face registered surprise, then feigned shock. "*Mister O'Leary!* I would never have expected an immoral proposition from such an esteemed member of the bar association."

Sean's mouth twitched. "*That* wasn't what I had in mind."

Erica stopped in midstep. "It wasn't?"

"Let's discuss it at your house," he said.

At her door a few minutes later, Erica kissed the key before inserting it into the lock.

"Should I be jealous?" Sean asked, but the question got lost in Erica's exuberant reaction as she entered the house.

"Hallelujah!" she said, throwing her hands in the air. "Home at last."

"Watch it," Sean said. "You're beginning to make me feel that my hospitality last night was wanting."

"It was anything but wanting," Erica said. "I'm just glad to be home after everything that happened."

"You have a message," Sean said, tilting his head toward the answering machine.

"Two," Erica observed, counting the blink sequence of the red light. "The phone rang last night when I was trying to find an unlocked window."

"Maybe you'd better listen."

"Why don't you just tell me what I'll hear," Erica said smugly. It was obvious from his demeanor that he knew exactly what was on the tape.

"It was a grovel call from your attorney," he said. "He said he'd made a big mistake and he was sorry and he hoped you and he could straighten things out because he missed you."

"And the second call?"

Sean shook his head. "More of the same. Pathetic groveling. Begging. Pleas for understanding and forgiveness."

Erica's eyes narrowed suspiciously. "Did you say these calls were from my attorney, or my lover?"

"It was from the attorney who loves you," Sean said.

"*Loves?*" Erica asked meekly, trying to absorb the full implications of the word.

"Well?" Sean prompted after a prolonged silence. "Don't keep me in suspense. What's the verdict, Miss O'Leary?"

She stepped into his arms and slid her arms around his waist. "I . . . think . . . I may love you, too."

"Think?" It wasn't the response he'd been hoping for.

"It's so complicated," she said. "I need time. It's not just between you and me. It's not even between you and me and your children. It's between you and your children, and me and the comfortable life I've established for myself since I took the teaching job at Suwannee. You can't ask me to—"

"All right," he said, reflexively hugging her tighter. "You're right. I would be asking you to make more changes than I'd have to make. I won't pressure you. I won't ask for anything right now except for you to keep an open mind and give us a chance."

Sighing, she let her cheek rest heavily against his chest. "I'd be crazy not to."

For a long time, they stayed that way, locked in a mutual embrace, silent by unspoken agreement. But, as good as it felt to be close to him that way, Erica knew they couldn't stay like that forever. Time stood still for no man and woman. Reluctantly, she said, "You wanted to discuss your fee?"

Sean dropped his arms from around her. "Let's sit down." After they'd settled on the sofa, he began, "Mrs. Smead called my office this morning. Her mother is stable, but she's facing an extended recovery with intensive therapy. Mrs. Smead is going to be in New Jersey several weeks."

"You can't want me to be your housekeeper," Erica said. "I told you, the laundry was only a favor."

"Laundry and cleaning are the least of my worries," Sean said. "I can do the laundry and call in a maid service. What I need is a nanny."

"A nanny?"

"I'm going to have to put the children in full-time day care if you don't help me out. I have two or three hourly baby-sitters who fill in from time to time, but they don't want full-time responsibility, and I've imposed on my sister long enough."

"I don't know if it's such a good idea, Sean."

"It makes perfect sense," Sean said. "I need someone to take care of the children, and you're a teacher. What could be more logical? It's not as though I'm asking you to leave a job and take this one."

Erica thought about her plans to read and watch movies. "This is the first summer I've taken off since I started teaching," she said. "I was looking forward to some leisure time to myself. And going through this house is going to take a lot of time and energy."

"It would give you and the children a chance to get acquainted," Sean said. "If things work out between us—"

"What happens if things don't work out between us?" Erica asked, locking her gaze with Sean's. "Isn't that what you try to protect your children from?"

"We'll keep our . . . *us* . . . private," he said. "You'll be presented as Mrs. Smead's temporary replacement. That way, they won't feel like you've been foisted on them in a like-it-or-not-she's-here-to-stay situation. And you can get to know them and see what you'd be getting yourself into if we—"

What? Erica wondered, overwhelmed by the ramifications. *If they got married? If she became the children's stepmother?*

"Whatever happens between us, I think you'd be good for the children," he said. "You understand kids better than Mrs. Smead. She takes excellent care of them. She keeps them clean and fed, but she's not a nurturer. She's more of a housekeeper who looks after children than a nanny."

He paused thoughtfully. "It's Kaitlin I'm most concerned about. I think she needs a woman who understands her. My sister's boys are eleven and nine. They tolerate Michael, but Kaitlin is always the outcast. My sister's sweet to her, but she's busy, and Kaitlin is only one of four when she's over there. She needs the type of one-on-one relationship I think you could give her."

"You're not fighting fair," Erica said. "Using Kaitlin—"

"I'm not using Kaitlin," Sean said. "I'm trying to get Kaitlin what she needs the most. And you're it."

Erica mulled over his words. "I won't sleep at your house, Sean," she said. "It's strictly a day job. If you and I decide to get together, it won't be in your house with the children in the next room."

"Fair enough," he said. "You're a nanny at my house. Anything else is off-site and private, after hours."

Erica leaned forward, bracing her hands on her thighs. "When do I start?"

Sean grimaced sheepishly. "How about now?"

Erica shook her head in exasperation. "How about after I change clothes and put on some real shoes?"

"How about kissing me before you change clothes?"

"How about kissing me and helping me change clothes?"

They didn't leave Erica's house for over an hour, and when they did, Sean was carrying the portrait of the flying pig under his arm.

14

"HOW DID YOU LEARN so much about plants?" Kaitlin asked.

"My grandmother taught me," Erica answered. "She and I used to work in the greenhouse together." She had brought Sean's children to the greenhouse to help Ardeth transplant seedlings from flats to individual pots.

Kaitlin poked another sprig of ivy into the soil in the clay pot she had prepared under Erica's supervision, first putting in a layer of pebbles to keep the drain hole clear and then filling it with potting soil. Erica watched her tamp the soil around the sprig with her small fingers exactly the way she'd been shown and felt a swell of love for the child. She'd been caring for Sean's children for two weeks now and already she felt a maternal tie to them.

So far, she and Sean had kept their relationship private, just as they'd agreed. As often as possible, he engaged baby-sitters to come to the house after the children were asleep so he could visit Erica. But it was getting more and more difficult to separate her relationship with Sean from her growing bond with his children. Each evening when she left Sean's house, it seemed a little more like leaving behind her own home and family. And the prospect of driving back to Georgia to step into the life she'd left there grew more remote every time she thought about it.

Her mind drifted to an overstuffed white envelope with the Suwannee Elementary School return address tucked away in her desk. Inside the envelope was a letter welcoming her

back, expressing the hopes that she had had a full and re-
warding summer vacation and calling her attention to the
enclosed schedule of the upcoming year and the agenda for
the teachers' orientation sessions and individual grade-level
team meetings to be held prior to the opening of school.

When she'd first opened the envelope and skimmed the text
of the cover letter, she'd realized that it wasn't a simple stack
of papers she held in her hand. It was an ultimatum.

Weeks. If she wanted to be fair to the principal and team
leader, that's how much time she had to decide whether she
would resign her teaching job. If she was not going back to
Georgia and Suwannee Elementary, it was only fair to notify
her principal in time to find a replacement for her, and it
would be easiest on everyone if a new teacher was hired prior
to the orientation and planning meetings.

Unfailingly, when she thought of her friends at Suwannee, of the students she'd come to love while teaching there,
of Gary and what a great friend he'd been to her, she immediately thought of Sean and his children. Of the sweet moments she and Sean shared when they were alone and
touching, and tender moments when they were with the
children, doing family things. Of Sean in the mornings, harried when she arrived at his house and found him trying to
take care of everyday things like making out checks to pay
his bills before he left for work.

And the children—grumpy little Michael, who wasn't
nearly as tough as he wanted everyone to think he was. And
not nearly as grumpy when he had something to do that excited him—like learning about the earthworm's role in soil
aeration...while holding one in his hand. Grubby from head
to toe, he was having the time of his life looking for worms
in the compost Ardeth had brought to the greenhouse, and
Ardeth was in her glory explaining the ecological value of

earthworms, lady bugs and other creepy, crawly critters in maintaining healthy soil and plants.

"Will this really grow all the way to the floor?" Kaitlin asked. The clippings she was planting were from an ivy Ardeth had pruned. Ardeth had explained that if the ivy was not pruned regularly, it would grow very, very long. Kaitlin had found the idea enchanting, and she was going to take the new pot home with her to see how long she could get the ivy to grow.

"It will if you take care of it," Erica said. "Plants are like people and pets—they need food and water and love."

"How do they eat? They don't have mouths."

Erica chuckled. "They eat with their feet—their roots take minerals out of the soil. That's why we have to keep the earth healthy. You'll learn all about it in science class one day."

"One hopes so," Ardeth said.

"You don't sound too convinced," Erica observed.

"City kids, busy parents, overworked teachers, crowded classrooms." Ardeth shrugged her shoulders in resignation. "It's a shame more kids don't have a chance to play in the soil like these children are playing today."

Erica clicked into teacher mode. "A hands-on greenhouse would make a marvelous field trip," she said. The idea settled in her brain like a seedling falling on fertile soil.

A little while later, Erica took the children into the backyard to wash their hands at the garden hose. What began as an accidental squirt that wet Michael's shirt culminated in a playful water war, with Erica chasing the children with the hose while they ran in circles around her, giggling and screeching. Later, she let them "steal" the hose from her and laughed until her eyes teared as they squirted her with the cold water. In the middle of the soggy conflict, she caught sight of Ardeth watching them, shaking her head and grinning.

As her gaze locked with Ardeth's, Erica was struck with sudden realization. *This was right. This was where she should be. This was what she should be doing. These children needed her, and she loved them, just as she loved their father.*

A FEW DAYS LATER, Sean arrived home from work to find Erica and the children clustered around one of the hedge bushes near the mailbox. "What are you guys looking at?" he asked.

"It's a spider," Michael replied excitedly. "A big one, with an awesome web."

Kaitlin, sitting cross-legged on the grass with a sketch pad in her lap, said excitedly, "I'm drawing a picture of it." She held the pad up so he could see her pencil sketch. "See?"

"That's great, Kaitlin," Sean said, looking from the picture to the spider centered on the web. "It looks just like it."

"Erica says she's seen lots of spiders, but she's never seen a web like this one. See? It has zigzags in it," Michael said. "Erica's going to take us to the library so we can get a book about spiders and find out what kind it is." His excitement escalated as he spoke. "And she isn't going to make us kill it. She says if we don't touch it, we can leave it right where it is and we can watch it catch bugs and stuff. She says if it's a female, it might even lay eggs, just like Charlotte."

"Charlotte who?" Sean asked.

"Daddy!" Kaitlin exclaimed, shaking her head. "You know who Charlotte is. In *Charlotte's Web.*"

"*Charlotte's Web.* Of course," Sean said. "Daddy just forgot."

"Erica's going to read us the book, and she says then we can rent the movie."

"It sounds as though you guys are going to be busy this week."

"We're always busy," Kaitlin said, turning her attention back to her sketch.

"Yes, you are," Sean said. "I've noticed that." He smiled at Erica above the children's heads. They'd been busy since Erica had taken over their care. She turned everything into an adventure for the children, beginning with a trip to the grocery store and fish market to buy everything they needed to surprise their father with a coddies dinner. He'd gotten a full report from both children on how they'd been allowed to use the potato masher to turn the boiled fish and potatoes into a mush, to pat the mixture into flat patties and then to keep a vigil on the coddies as they fried, letting Erica know when the coddies were ready to be turned. After buying corn and tomatoes from a roadside vendor, they'd been allowed to shuck the corn and tear lettuce into small pieces to toss in a salad with the tomatoes.

They'd done a chalk mural on the driveway, documented a day in their lives with disposable cameras and enrolled in the library's summer reading program. They'd taken the cat to the veterinarian for shots and come home with a tale of the gigantic dog they'd met in the waiting room.

Day by day Sean grew more convinced that Erica belonged with him and the kids. It was not merely the convenience of having a woman's nurturing presence in his children's lives that convinced him, nor was it his deep, abiding love for Erica which deepened with each passing hour. It was that Erica herself was flourishing. Her growing affection for the children was written in her soft smiles as she hugged or praised them, in her patience when she was forced to be strict with them, in the catch in her voice when he and she were alone and she related some funny or touching anecdote about something one of the children had said or done.

By silent, mutual consent, they did not speak of the future. He'd promised not to pressure her, but the weight of that promise increased in proportion to his love for her. She *belonged* with them. He just had to give her time to realize it for herself.

He was growing weary of waiting until the children went to bed and driving to her house like a man having a clandestine affair. They made love on his visits and talked, sharing their innermost thoughts. But, always, he had to get up and go home. He could not hold her all night, the way he had the first time he met her. He could not go to sleep listening to her breathe, knowing she was safe. He could not spontaneously pull her into his arms and hug her in front of the children.

On the night of the day the children found the spider, he visited Erica. As they lay together in the afterglow of lovemaking, she said, "The children enjoyed working in the greenhouse the other day."

Sean nodded. "Kaitlin is like a lioness fretting over a cub with that ivy."

Erica smiled. "I have to keep reminding her that it needs to dry out between waterings. She'd drown it if she watered it as often as she asks if it needs it."

"She's convinced it's grown every time she looks at it," Sean said.

Affection enriched Erica's voice. "She wants it to grow all the way to the floor."

"Listen to us," Sean said, curling his arm tighter around her. "We sound like parents."

"You *are* a parent."

"I said par*ents*," he said, emphasizing the last syllable. "Plural."

Her eyes closed as she sighed. "They're so easy to love, Sean. They're so—"

She didn't need to finish the thought. He shared her sentiment. Sean hugged her closer.

After a mellow silence, Erica said, "I've been thinking about the house."

Sean's guts tightened as he waited for her to continue.

"I don't want to give it up," she said. "Not entirely. When the kids were here, digging and playing with earthworms, and Ardeth was explaining soil aeration to Michael, it occurred to me—"

She paused to take a breath. "Do you think we could get zoning permits to convert the house into a horticultural center for children?"

"Horticultural center?"

"A place where children could come to learn about how things grow. We could convert the larger rooms inside the house into classrooms and use the smaller ones for offices, and use the greenhouse as a lab for hands-on learning. I know I could get the Green Thumbs involved."

"I'll check into the zoning tomorrow. I don't think there'll be a problem as long as the center doesn't disrupt the neighborhood. You might have to put in a special parking area—"

"And a second greenhouse, with lower worktables," she said excitedly. "The Marian Stonehouse Memorial Horticultural Center for Children. Please check, Sean. As soon as possible. We could announce the plans at the tree dedication next week. It would be the perfect time for it. All the Green Thumbs will be there." The tree honoring her grandmother would be planted and the memorial plaque unveiled on her grandmother's birthday.

Erica's forehead creased as she looked at Sean's face. "What are you grinning about?"

"We," he said. "I like the sound of it." He loved seeing her so animated and excited—especially about a project that would likely keep her in Baltimore.

"So do I," she said. "I'm so glad you and the children will be with me." She had been asked to make a formal acknowledgment of the dedication and, though she was accustomed to speaking in front of students, she knew she would need emotional support at this event.

THE NEWS of the establishment of the Marian Stonehouse Memorial Horticultural Center for Children—to be known informally as The Growing Place—was greeted with enthusiasm. Many of the Green Thumbs expressed an interest in helping with the project, either by teaching classes or helping children pot seedlings. Erica was exhilarated as Sean drove her and the children back to the house after the dedication ceremony in the town square.

Michael showed his usual grumpiness, complaining that the ceremony had been long and boring. "Bor-ing," with two syllables.

Kaitlin was unusually quiet. Erica found out what was on the little girl's mind later that afternoon when Kaitlin looked at her and asked, "Why do people plant trees for dead people?"

"It's a way of honoring them," Erica replied. "The tree is a living thing, and as it grows, it makes the earth prettier and the air fresher. And when people see the tree, they feel better."

"I don't think my mother has a tree."

"Not all dead people do," Erica said. "Just the ones whose loved ones choose to remember them in that special way."

"Could I remember my mother if I planted a tree for her?"

Erica's heart nearly burst with empathy for Kaitlin at that moment. She knew what it was to be the only little girl in school without a mother, without even memories of one.

"Planting a tree wouldn't give you memories of your mother," she said, "but it would help you remember that she was a person who loved you and cared for you and Michael and your daddy."

She watched the child digest that idea and waited for the inevitable question. Kaitlin did not keep her in suspense long. "Could I plant a tree for my mother?"

"I think that would be a wonderful thing for you to do," Erica replied. "Do you want me to talk to your daddy and see what he thinks of the idea?"

Kaitlin nodded and then threw herself into Erica's arms. Erica hugged her tightly. "I didn't have a mother, either, Kaitlin. My mother died when I was just a baby."

Later, when she broached the subject with Sean, he asked her opinion about the wisdom of the idea. "I think it would be good for Kaitlin," she said. "Right now, her mother is just a phantom figure people tell her about. She knows she's *supposed* to love her, but it's hard when she has no memories to hold on to. The gesture of planting a tree might allow her to deal not only with the fact that her mother is dead, but also enable her to establish a link to her mother that makes her feel as though she's been a dutiful daughter."

Sean's face reflected anguish. "I never realized—"

"You couldn't be expected to understand Kaitlin's detachment when you were so totally involved with your own grieving process."

"You understood," he said, studying her face.

"I can't remember my mother, either."

He wrapped his arms around her and pressed her cheek against his chest, cradling her head in his large hand. "I knew Kaitlin needed you as much as I do."

THEY PLANTED THE TREE when Sean returned home from work the next day. Kaitlin had carried the easel from her room out to the planting site and put a small picture of her mother on it, the way Erica's grandmother's portrait had been displayed at the memorial.

After Sean helped the children tamp the soil around the base of the tree, he moved to Erica's side while the children conducted a brief ceremony. For a young man who'd found the dedication "bor-ing," Michael must have been paying close attention to the proceedings, because he stepped into the role of master of ceremonies with panache. Kaitlin made a sweet, plaintive speech about how her mother had been pretty, and the tree would be pretty.

Halfway through the children's presentation, Sean reached for Erica's hand and squeezed it.

That night, Erica telephoned Gary to tell him she had written her letter of resignation from Suwannee Elementary. "I didn't want you to hear it from anyone else," she said.

Her next call was to the principal, to let her know she should watch for the letter in the mail.

WHILE ERICA WAS MAKING the phone calls that closed a chapter of her life, Sean was talking to his housekeeper on the phone at his house. The call was only a few minutes long. After hanging up, Sean debated who he should talk it over with first—Erica or the children. Michael helped settle the matter when he looked Sean in the eye and asked, "Who was that?"

"It was Mrs. Smead," Sean said, watching his children closely for their reactions. "Her mother is better. She'll be coming back to Towson next week."

The children were quiet. Too quiet. Sean let them mull over the news a moment before asking, "What's wrong?"

"Does that mean Erica won't be our nanny anymore?" Kaitlin asked.

"I don't want Mrs. Smead to come back," Michael said. "If she sees Fritzi's web, she'll tear it down and then she'll stomp on Fritzi and squish her."

"We'll make sure that doesn't happen," Sean said. "I'll explain about Fritzi."

Michael appeared unconvinced. "Mrs. Smead *hates* spiders. She thinks they're all poison, but they're not."

"Why don't you ask Erica to come live with us?" Kaitlin said. "She could be our mommy."

Sean's heart skipped a beat, especially when Michael said, "Well, duh, Kaitlin. Erica couldn't be our mother unless she married Daddy, and people don't get married unless they're in love."

Sean struggled to keep a straight face. Michael was so young to be so wise! "What if I said that I was in love with Erica? How would you feel if I asked her to marry me and live with us and be your mother?"

He held his breath waiting on their answers.

Michael shrugged his shoulders. "I guess it would be okay. I mean, she wouldn't let Mrs. Smead squish Fritzi."

Kaitlin, eyes large and earnest, blurted out, "Will you call her on the phone and ask her right now? Please?"

Laughing, Sean scooped his daughter into his arms. "That's not the way it's done, Kaitlin. A woman likes music and flowers and candlelight when a man asks her to marry him."

"We have candles," Kaitlin said. "'Member? Mrs. Smead keeps them in the drawer for when the 'lectricity goes off."

"That's not the kind of candles we need."

"Then let's go buy the right kind," Kaitlin said.

Sean didn't understand why he hadn't been the one to think of it. "Why not?" he said. "The stores are still open. Let's go get everything we need, and you two can help me ask her in the morning."

When Erica entered the house at seven-thirty the next morning, she couldn't believe her eyes. The family room was filled with flowers, and the glow of candlelight softened the morning sunshine coming through the windows. "What?" she asked, turning to Sean with a blank look on her face.

"Surprise!" shouted Kaitlin and Michael, jumping up from where they'd been crouched behind the sofa hiding, waiting to surprise her.

"What's going on?" Erica asked, although, deep in her heart, she already knew.

"This is an ambush," Sean said. "The children have something to ask you."

"Will you marry Daddy and be our mommy?" Kaitlin asked, offering Erica a nosegay of daisies tied with long satin ribbons.

All eyes fell to Michael who, with his hands behind his back, twirled his toe in the carpet self-consciously, looking as if he had something on his mind.

"It's okay with me," he finally conceded. "I wouldn't mind having a mother. All the other kids do." With that off his chest, he took his hands from behind his back and presented her with a rose.

"Will you?" Kaitlin asked.

"That depends," Erica said, looking at Sean. "We haven't heard from your father yet."

"It's okay with him," Michael said.

Erica touched the tip of the boy's nose with the rose. "I think I'd like to hear it from him."

Blushing like an adolescent, Sean knelt in front of her and took the bouquet from her hands and gave it back to Kaitlin so he could hold Erica's hand as he gazed into her eyes. "Erica Susan O'Leary, I love you. My children love you. We want you to be part of our lives and part of our family. If you'll do me the honor of being my wife, I promise to love and cherish you and take care of you. Will you marry us?"

"Please," Kaitlin said, her face strained with earnestness. "You wouldn't have to change your name. It's already O'Leary."

"If you don't, Mrs. Smead might stomp on Fritzi," Michael added.

"Well?" Sean prompted.

Erica laughed through her tears. "How could any woman refuse a proposal like that?"

Epilogue

"ARE WE REALLY GOING to be in Florida when we wake up?" Kaitlin said.

"Yes," Erica replied. The children were excited about the trip, but Erica knew from experience that if they ever settled down, the rocking of the sleeper car would lull them to sleep in no time.

"It sounds like *The Little Engine that Could*," Kaitlin said, referring to the little train engine who chugged, "I think I can. I think I can," while pulling the rest of the train up a hill.

"Yes, it does," Erica agreed.

"Are we really going to see Mickey Mouse and Buzz Lightyear?" Kaitlin asked, her voice growing faint.

"Well, duh! Yes!" Michael said. "And we're going to see a killer whale, and sharks, and alligators, and NASA—"

"You two are not going to see anything if you don't get some sleep," Sean said. "You'll be too tired to go anywhere."

"These are funny beds," Kaitlin said with a soft giggle.

"They're not really beds," Michael said. "Beds don't pull down from the wall."

"Beds on trains do," Kaitlin said, rolling into a sleep position as she clutched her favorite stuffed bear.

Erica kissed the children one last time and tucked their bedding around them before joining Sean.

"I thought you'd never get here, Mrs. O'Leary," Sean whispered, his body spooning with hers on the narrow mattress as he hugged her close. They'd been married in a simple ceremony in the church where Erica's mother had been christened. Michael and Kaitlin had been best man and maid of honor, Sean's sister and brother-in-law had been their official witnesses.

"They're excited," Erica said, referring to the children.

"So am I," Sean said, grinning.

They would have privacy in their hotel suite in Orlando. For now, they were restricted to quiet cuddling in the small compartment they shared with the children. "It's sweet torture, isn't it?" Erica said.

"It was the first time, too," Sean said. *More than she would ever know.*

National Bestselling Author

JoAnn Ross

Welcomes you to Raintree, Georgia—
steamy capital of sin, scandal and murder.

Southern Comforts

Chelsea Cassidy is the official biographer of
Roxanne Scarbrough—the Southern Queen of good
taste who's built an empire around the how-to's of
gracious living. It's clear to Chelsea that somebody
wants her employer dead.

As Chelsea explores the dark secrets of Roxanne's
life, the search leads Chelsea into the arms of
Cash Beaudine. And now her investigating becomes
personal with potentially fatal consequences.

Available this September wherever books are sold.

REBECCA

43 LIGHT STREET

YORK

FACE TO FACE

Bestselling author Rebecca York returns to "43 Light Street"
for an original story of past secrets, deadly deceptions—and
the most intimate betrayal.

She woke in a hospital—with amnesia…and with child.
According to her rescuer, whose striking face is the last
image she remembers, she's Justine Hollingsworth. But
nothing about her life seems to fit, except for the baby
inside her and Mike Lancer's arms around her. Consumed
by forbidden passion and racked by nameless fear, she
must discover if she is Justine…or the victim of some mind
game. Her life—and her unborn child's—depends on it….

Don't miss *Face To Face*—Available in October, wherever
Harlequin books are sold.

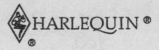

HARLEQUIN ®

43FTF

A woman with a shocking secret.
A man without a past.
Together, their love could be nothing less than

Scandalous

The latest romantic adventure from

CANDACE CAMP

When a stranger suffering a loss of memory lands on Priscilla Hamilton's doorstep, her carefully guarded secret is threatened. Always a model of propriety, she knows that no one would believe the deep, dark desire that burns inside her at this stranger's touch.

As scandal and intrigue slowly close in on the lovers, will their attraction be strong enough to survive?

Find out this September at your favorite retail outlet.

MIRA **The brightest star in women's fiction**   MCCSC

Look us up on-line at:http://www.romance.net

Merry Christmas, Baby!

A romantic collection filled with the magic of Christmas and the joy of children.

SUSAN WIGGS, Karen Young and Bobby Hutchinson bring you Christmas wishes, weddings and romance, in a charming trio of stories that will warm up your holiday season.

MERRY CHRISTMAS, BABY! also contains Harlequin's special gift to you—a set of FREE GIFT TAGS included in every book.

Brighten up your holiday season with *MERRY CHRISTMAS, BABY!*

Available in November at your favorite retail store.

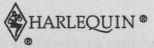

HARLEQUIN ®

Look us up on-line at: http://www.romance.net   MCB

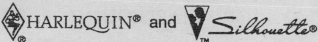

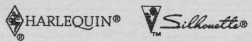

HARLEQUIN®

Don't miss these Harlequin favorites by some of our most distinguished authors!
And now, you can receive a discount by ordering two or more titles!

HT #25663	THE LAWMAN by Vicki Lewis Thompson	$3.25 U.S. ☐/$3.75 CAN. ☐
HP #11788	THE SISTER SWAP by Susan Napier	$3.25 U.S. ☐/$3.75 CAN. ☐
HR #03293	THE MAN WHO CAME FOR CHRISTMAS by Bethany Campbell	$2.99 U.S. ☐/$3.50 CAN. ☐
HS #70667	FATHERS & OTHER STRANGERS by Evelyn Crowe	$3.75 U.S. ☐/$4.25 CAN. ☐
HI #22198	MURDER BY THE BOOK by Margaret St. George	$2.89 ☐
HAR #16520	THE ADVENTURESS by M.J. Rodgers	$3.50 U.S. ☐/$3.99 CAN. ☐
HH #28885	DESERT ROGUE by Erin Yorke	$4.50 U.S. ☐/$4.99 CAN. ☐

(limited quantities available on certain titles)

	AMOUNT	$
DEDUCT:	**10% DISCOUNT FOR 2+ BOOKS**	$
ADD:	**POSTAGE & HANDLING**	$
	($1.00 for one book, 50¢ for each additional)	
	APPLICABLE TAXES**	$_____
	TOTAL PAYABLE	$_____
	(check or money order—please do not send cash)	

To order, complete this form and send it, along with a check or money order for the total above, payable to Harlequin Books, to: **In the U.S.:** 3010 Walden Avenue, P.O. Box 9047, Buffalo, NY 14269-9047; **In Canada:** P.O. Box 613, Fort Erie, Ontario, L2A 5X3.

Name: _____

Address: _____ City: _____

State/Prov.: _____ Zip/Postal Code: _____

**New York residents remit applicable sales taxes.
  Canadian residents remit applicable GST and provincial taxes.

HBACK-JS3

Look us up on-line at: http://www.romance.net